"Stripping is work.

"I'm not a hooker and I don't strip bare. I've only done it a few times. I needed that money." She swallowed. When was the last time she'd had something to eat or drink?

She was suddenly so tired, so sick of fighting to eke out an existence. Still, she pressed on. "You wouldn't know what it's like to be poor, would you? You wouldn't know how hard it is to make sure your child doesn't suffer. You wouldn't know—" She suddenly saw two Dr. Quinton Searles. How could that be?

Both Quintons spoke. "Beth, you don't look so good. You're pale and—"

"I'm fine," Beth said. She was always fine. She couldn't afford not to be.

And then, as if fate mocked her, the world went black.

Dear Reader,

As a parent of young children, I can't tell you how many times I've been in the emergency room. My oldest daughter once got into my purse and ate my cold medicine thinking it was candy, and my youngest daughter once fell and bit completely through her lower lip. These motherhood experiences of mine provided the backdrop for Beth Johnson and Quinton Searle's love story.

Quinton first appeared as a minor character in my July 2002 Harlequin American Romance release, *Catching the Corporate Playboy*. The minute I wrote him I knew he needed his own book. I decided he'd be perfect for Beth, a woman who's been through some pretty rough times in her life but is determined to survive. While she doesn't need a prince in a doctor's coat to rescue her, her life is a lot more enjoyable and fun once he does. Of course, Beth's daughter, Carly, has a few ideas of her own about the man she wants to be her next daddy.

I hope you enjoy reading Quinton and Beth's tale as much as I did writing it.

All the best and as always, enjoy the romance.

Michele Dunaway

EMERGENCY ENGAGEMENT

Michele Dunaway

HARLEQUIN®

TORONTO • NEW YORK • LONDON
AMSTERDAM • PARIS • SYDNEY • HAMBURG
STOCKHOLM • ATHENS • TOKYO • MILAN • MADRID
PRAGUE • WARSAW • BUDAPEST • AUCKLAND

ISBN 0-373-75060-9

EMERGENCY ENGAGEMENT

Copyright © 2005 by Michele Dunaway.

www.eHarlequin.com

Printed in U.S.A.

To Julie Picraux, romance reader extraordinaire;
Eutana Howard, Susan Benedict, Alexandra Gantner
and Joyce Adams Counts. I am honored that
I can call all of you my friends.

And to Kenny Chesney,
whose music and dedication to it are inspirations.

Books by Michele Dunaway

Don't miss any of our special offers. Write to us at the
following address for information on our newest releases.

Harlequin Reader Service
U.S.: 3010 Walden Ave., P.O. Box 1325, Buffalo, NY 14269
Canadian: P.O. Box 609, Fort Erie, Ont. L2A 5X3

Chapter One

He wasn't supposed to be there. It wasn't his night; in fact, this week he wasn't supposed to deal with *any* emergencies unless they occurred during normal office hours.

But because of a wedding or something like that, there'd been a shortage of pediatricians to staff the pediatric emergency floor. So when his partner Bart had asked, Quinton had agreed to take Bart's shift. Even though it was a Friday night, Quinton had had nothing better to do.

Which, when he stopped to think about it, was pathetic. He, Dr. Quinton Searle, pediatric specialist, *should* have something to do. At thirty-five, he should have some woman to date, some place to be.

But the truth was that he didn't, which is why, when the call came through, he was in the wrong place at the right time. He turned to Elaine, who at fifty-something had seen it all. He liked working with her; she was a model of efficiency, the most reliable nurse in any crisis. "What have I got?" he asked.

"Four-year-old child. Poison Control just called. The kid ate the mother's cold medicine. Thought it was green candy."

He frowned as he contemplated the situation. "How many?"

Elaine checked her notes. "The mother thinks it was only two tablets, but she isn't sure. The container is empty."

Great. Quinton hated variables. "Is she here yet?"

Elaine shook her head. "Any minute. Downstairs knows to buzz me immediately so we can bring the kid right up."

Quinton nodded. *Downstairs* was slang for the main emergency room. As part of the Chicago Presbyterian Hospital's patient care plan, a separate emergency floor had been set up especially for children. Children were triaged in the main ER, then sent to the pediatric ER. Even admittance paperwork could be done on this floor. He shoved his hand into the pocket of his white doctor's coat. "Let me know the minute you get the buzz."

"Will do," Elaine replied. "I'm going to check on the patient in room twelve. The pediatric plastic surgeon should have been here twenty minutes ago."

"Good idea," Quinton said. When he had phoned earlier, the surgeon had assured Quinton that he'd be there in ten minutes. Already half an hour had passed.

Which was not good. The three-year-old boy waiting for the surgeon had fallen completely through the skin below his lower lip. Fifteen minutes ago the parents had given up keeping the numbing cream on the injury. That, of course, meant the cream would have worn off somewhat by the time the surgeon finally arrived.

Quinton frowned. Besides coping with variables, he hated waiting on specialists. He could have stitched up the injury himself, but probably not without leaving a worse scar than the plastic surgeon would. So, since Quinton knew the kid needed both internal and external stitches, he and the family were both waiting. Not an ideal situation at all, and now his time would be further divided when the drug overdose arrived.

He could use some caffeine. Having a few spare moments, he went to the staff lounge and filled a white foam cup with hot coffee. Someone had made a fresh pot, and the aroma wafted toward his nose as he sipped. The bitter black balm failed to soothe his soul. He contemplated the real reason he'd chosen to work this weekend.

Bart and responsibilities as a member of the hospital staff aside, work had gotten him out of a family function relating to his sister's upcoming wedding. Not that he didn't love his parents or his only sibling, but he didn't necessarily want to see them, or hear the question they always asked: when was he moving home for good?

Trouble was, he didn't want to return to St. Louis. The staff lounge window overlooked parts of Chicago, a city he'd called home since attending medical school at Northwestern University, and Quinton paused a moment to study the darkened cityscape. Chicago vibrated with life, and the city had a way of neutralizing differences. In St. Louis, life was all about where you went to high school and what country club you joined after college.

In Chicago, no one in his current social circle cared. In Chicago, he wasn't Fred Searle's son, groomed since birth to take over his aging father's still-thriving medical practice. His parents had it all planned: Quinton was to marry the right girl, join the right club and have his kids attend the right schools. He'd assume his rightful place in St. Louis society.

But St. Louis society stifled; it didn't foster growth as did Chicago's eclectic mix. In his opinion, St. Louis had no real diversity, except for perhaps racially mixed University City, a town that Quinton's family saw as too liberal and certainly not a fitting place for their grown son.

In Chicago, he was free from all that. Free from the mistakes he'd made, the people he'd inadvertently hurt in his crueler high school days. In his new hometown he could disappear into anonymity, or he could join what he wanted. There wasn't one museum to visit but several. And the best part of Chicago was the magnificent Lake Michigan lakeshore, that expanse of blue water that never failed to calm him. He was a Cancer, a crab; he needed water. His apartment had floor-to-ceiling windows that gave him a view of the lake from two sides. When looking out over the lake toward Indiana, Quinton almost felt as if he could fly. Better yet, during the summer he could pull his boat out of its mooring and disappear into the endless blue.

But June was still five months away.

He tossed the empty cup into the trash can, the brew having somehow disappeared during his reverie. He didn't remember drinking the coffee.

The lounge door shot inward, and Elaine poked her head through. "They're downstairs," she announced. "Jena is getting them now."

CARLY JOHNSON wanted to cry. She hated hospitals. Hated them the way she hated lima beans.

Her daddy had died in a hospital.

"Shh." Her mommy leaned over and held her tight while carrying her through the double doors.

Carly felt somewhat safer. She had a good mommy; that she knew. Mommy's arms were always soft, always open. Mommy really wasn't *angry* with her for getting into her purse. No, Carly thought as the bright lights assaulted her face, her mommy was more worried than anything.

Carly could always tell when her mommy worried because her blond eyebrows would pucker together and her blue eyes would darken. She'd overheard her aunt Ida saying something to her mommy about working too hard for her twenty-six years. Carly knew her mommy had to be old because she herself could only count to twenty without tripping over some numbers. Her head spun a little as she blinked back the light and tried to focus on what the nurse was saying.

She wore a coat covered with teddy bears. Carly liked teddy bears.

"How many did she take?"

"I think only two, but I'm not sure."

Carly frowned at her mommy's answer. Her mommy didn't sound quite right.

"Well, let's get her right upstairs. We have a room already waiting for her. We'll photocopy your insurance card up there."

With that Carly felt her mommy's arms tighten. Life hadn't been too easy with Daddy gone. Her mommy worked long hours at Luie's, baking all sorts of things. Carly got a lot of leftover cookies, but because money was tight, she really didn't have lots of toys and extras. Not like Sarah, their new neighbor in the third-floor condo. Sarah had everything: toys, cookies *and* candy.

That was why Carly had eaten the pretty green pills when she'd found them in Mommy's purse. She'd actually been after lipstick for a dress-up game, but it seemed so long since she'd had any candy. The last time had been Christmas; and Easter, when mommy always gave her a big chocolate bunny, was nowhere in sight.

"Mommy?" Carly asked suddenly. Being four, she could ask big girl questions.

"Yes, darling?"

Mommy appeared close to tears. Carly wished Mommy didn't have to worry so much.

"Mommy? Am I going to heaven like Daddy?"

FIFTY DOLLARS. Beth Johnson knew her medical insurance's emergency room co-pay by heart, and unfortunately, while she had the heart to pay for her daughter's treatment, Beth didn't have fifty dollars. Every bit of her meager resources from her twelve-dollar-an-hour job was allocated to bills, food and more bills. But for her daughter's sake—for Carly certainly didn't need to see how worried her mother was—Beth had to keep a reassuring smile plastered on her face. Just once, though, Beth wished someone would reassure *her*— tell *her* that everything would be okay and that in twelve days they'd have somewhere besides a homeless shelter to live.

"Here we are," the nurse said as the elevator doors opened. "You'll be in room three, Carly. We call it the Butterfly Room because it has pictures of butterflies painted on the walls."

"Really?" Carly asked. She wiggled her way out of Beth's arms.

"Really," the nurse said. She pointed to a doorway. "Here, come see for yourself."

Beth watched as Carly bounded into the room. Anyone looking at her daughter wouldn't think she'd done anything wrong. In fact, Beth hadn't thought so, either, until she'd seen the thin, telltale green circle around Carly's mouth. Carly had denied everything, but a quick check of her tongue had confirmed Beth's worst fears— that Carly had eaten the green cold medicine. The push-through plastic had been empty, and for the life of her, Beth couldn't remember how many pills had been left.

At least the pediatric ER rooms weren't like those downstairs. Beth had seen enough of those cold, sterile rooms to last her a lifetime. Here, at least, the rooms had colorful murals on the walls. Carly was currently counting green butterflies and the nurse had put a Disney princess movie in before she'd left.

"Hello, Carly, I'm Nurse Elaine." A new nurse stepped into the room. Unlike her younger counterpart's, Elaine's scrubs were bright pink. "Let me take a look at you. Can you put this thermometer under your tongue for me?" Elaine held out a wand attached to a spiral cord, which was then connected to a rectangular device the nurse held in her other hand. Carly opened her mouth. "See, I knew you could. You are such a big girl."

The thermometer beeped and Elaine withdrew it. "No fever. That's a great sign."

Relief filled Beth.

"Now, Carly, your doctor is named Dr. Searle. It's like *girl* only with an *S*."

"Searle," Carly said dutifully.

"Very good," Elaine said. "He's going to be right in. You enjoy your movie. I like this one."

"Me, too," Carly said. She began to clap and sing as the characters performed a musical number.

Elaine stepped toward Beth. "Have you recalled how many she took?"

Beth shook her head. "No."

"Well, Dr. Searle will be in shortly. We have an injury requiring stitching and he's consulting with the plastic surgeon. If your daughter's condition changes in any way, push this call button."

"Okay." Beth focused her attention first on the call button and, after Elaine left, to the movie. Not even two minutes went by before she noticed a movement outside the doorway.

And when Carly's doctor stepped in, Beth decided that it really was one of the worst days of her life.

Dr. Quinton Searle—for that was what was stitched on his white coat—was gazing right through her, his concentration on her child.

"Hi, Carly," Dr. Searle said. "Hi, Carly's mom."

"Hi, Dr. Searle!" Carly said.

"Did you read my name?" He pointed to the blue stitching above his heart.

"No! Elaine taught it to me."

"You're smart and honest," he said. He went over to her. "I like smart and honest. You're pretty, too."

Carly giggled and her cheeks reddened. Even she wasn't immune to Dr. Searle's charm.

"So you ate some green medicine."

"It was a bad thing to do," Carly said with a solemn nod.

"Very bad," Dr. Searle agreed.

Carly blinked once at his serious tone. "Am I going to die?"

His hand stilled from taking a tongue depressor out of a clear plastic dispenser and he frowned slightly. "No. Of course not. Why would you think that?"

"Because my daddy died in a hospital. He had cancer."

He shook his head. "Of course not. You won't die. You swallowed some medicine that you shouldn't have, but your mommy brought you in here and I'm going to make you as good as new. To do that, though, I have to do some tests. Can you stick out your tongue for me?"

Beth remained standing as the doctor performed a series of tests. Carly's response to him pained her. She'd known that her four-year-old daughter missed her father, but she hadn't realized until now how much Carly missed simple male attention.

Beth missed it, too, but she was all grown up and understood that the world wasn't fair.

Carly didn't.

"Well, Carly, I think I have a solution to your problem. I'll definitely be able to fix you all up," said Quinton.

Carly gave him a hopeful smile. "Really?"

"Really," Dr. Quinton Searle said returning Carly's grin.

Then his expression grew serious. "But it won't be pleasant. In fact, you'll need to drink something that tastes pretty bad."

"I can do it!" Carly's blond pigtail bobbed as she nodded.

"I bet you will. I'll have Elaine get the special drink. I'll be right back."

"Okay." Carly watched as he left. Her blue eyes remained wide as she turned to her mother. "He's as handsome as Prince Eric, don't you think, Mommy? They have the same dark hair."

"I think Princess Ariel is a very lucky lady," Beth said, sidestepping the question. She didn't have to look too long at Dr. Quinton Searle to see he fit "tall, dark and handsome" to a tee. She estimated his height at six foot three, and under the white coat she could tell he had broad shoulders that tapered to a slim waist. Even Randy at his peak hadn't been so physically fit.

"Princess Ariel is lucky," Carly agreed.

Beth reached out and brushed her daughter's bangs away from her forehead. "You're lucky, too, if all you have to do is drink some special liquid."

Carly nodded. "I know. I'm sorry, Mommy."

"I love you," Beth said.

"Me, too! Oh, look, here's where Prince Eric saves Ariel from the Sea Witch!"

Beth smiled slightly, glad that Carly's attention was diverted. Too bad there weren't real princes who came in to save princesses. Not that Beth thought of herself as a princess. Princesses didn't have dull dishwater-blond hair, tired blue eyes, and five extra pounds on their hips. And her prince had died before fully saving her, if he had ever been going to save her at all.

She had to get over her melancholy. She couldn't fault Randy for her daily struggle; she could only fault herself. She'd been the one to insist they get married when she discovered she was pregnant. Would their marriage have survived had he lived? She didn't know, and worrying about it now was pointless.

"Here's your special drink." Elaine was back with a big white foam cup. A colorful straw extended past the plastic lid.

Carly clapped her hands. "The straw bends!" Carly said. "We never get bendy straws at our house."

"Well, this one does, and you may bend it," Elaine said.

"Is my drink chocolate?"

"No, but it is dark," Elaine answered. "And I'm going to stay here while you drink all of it." She handed Carly the cup. "Carly, Dr. Searle needs to see your mommy for a moment. She's going to meet him in a room down the hall."

"Okay," Carly said. She took a drink and grimaced.

Beth realized that her daughter was putting on a brave front when Carly said, "This isn't too bad."

"Well, there's a lot of it to drink," Elaine said.

"I can do it!" Carly said. She took another pull on the straw.

Elaine turned her attention back to Beth. "The small lounge, three doors down on the left."

"Thank you. Carly, I'll be right back."

Carly, her mouth full of drink, just nodded.

When Beth arrived at the small lounge, Dr. Searle wasn't present. She studied the beige, nondescript room. Here the touches done for children vanished; in their place was the austere environment so character-istic of hospitals.

"Mrs. Johnson?"

She faced him. "Yes."

As the doctor stepped into the room, Beth's hand automatically touched her hair. Not that she should worry about how she appeared. But suddenly she knew exactly how pathetic she must appear—how horribly inadequate as a mother, how totally unfeminine. Over a year had passed since she'd had a professional haircut, and her long hair was held back from her face with a plain black headband. She hated disarray, which was literally her life of late.

And this man was a physician, with years of college, whereas she'd had none. Worse, he was one of those attractive, self-assured men who exuded presence. She braced herself. Even though she probably had nothing to fear, her gut tightened anyway.

"I wanted to speak with you about Carly's treatment where she couldn't overhear us."

"That's fine."

"Can I get you some coffee or something? Water?"

He poured himself a cup, and for a moment Beth was tempted. But coffee was a luxury, and it was better to avoid what she couldn't have again. "Water, please," she said.

He set down his cup and poured her some water. He held the cup out for her, and their fingers connected as he transferred it to her hand. A gorgeous-man's touch. Beth shivered slightly. His eyes narrowed and she could now see how gray they were.

"Cold?" he asked.

"Just worried," Beth said.

"Don't be. Carly is currently drinking what amounts, in layman's terms, to liquid charcoal. The charcoal will act as a sponge and absorb the medicine. From there it will travel quickly through her system and be expelled as fecal matter."

She must have frowned, for he said, "It'll hit her hard and she'll have several loose bowel movements. After she's had the first, we'll release her. Unless you notice any behavior—such as sluggishness or hyperactivity—that is out of the ordinary, we won't need to see her again. However, you should consult with her pediatrician tomorrow morning, as well, just in case he wants you to follow up with a visit."

"Okay."

"That's it." He turned to leave.

An odd panic consumed Beth. Maybe his impersonal demeanor had gotten to her, or maybe it was just her overwhelming guilt—that she should have put her purse out of reach, that somehow she should have been more careful, more vigilant. She had to make him understand.

"I didn't leave my purse out. I didn't even know she had it, or that she was into it."

He gave her an accepting smile, as if he heard such excuses all the time. If Beth wanted sympathy, she didn't get it. Empathy came, instead.

"She's a child. Children do things like this. She'll probably be stronger for it after learning from her mistake. You can remind her of it when she's a teenager."

Beth followed him from the room. He quickly out-distanced her and she soon learned why. From down the hall she could hear Carly complaining, "I don't want to drink any more. It's yucky. I'm full."

The doctor stepped inside her daughter's room. "I hear you're full."

His voice rumbled over Beth and she heard the easy manner with which he handled Carly.

"Uh-huh. I'm full," Carly repeated.

As Beth reached the doorway, Quinton took the cup from Elaine's hand. He lifted the lid and checked the amount. He shook his head. "Carly, Carly. And you told me you'd drink it all."

His voice was teasing, and pain filled Beth. With his sickness, Randy had been unable to reach Carly on her level. Yet Dr. Searle succeeded with masterful ease. Why couldn't Beth have found a man like that?

"It's yucky," Carly said. "My belly hurts."

He peered into the cup again. "How about a deal? You drink half of what's left and I'll throw the rest away."

"Half?" Carly's face had the hopefulness and skepticism of a child debating whether to eat liver.

"Half." Dr. Searle took a pen from his pocket and drew a black line around the outside of the cup. "Right here. A few good sips should do it. In fact, I'll wait. Do you think you can give me three good sips?"

Carly had brightened. "Yes." She reached for the cup, and he held it as she sucked on the straw.

"One." He counted. Carly stopped for a break. Quinton shook the cup. "Two more."

Carly took another deep drag on the straw, and Beth's heart wrenched as her daughter's face scrunched up.

"That was great," he said. "One more, Carly. You can do it."

Carly must have caught some of his enthusiasm, for she said, "I can do it," and went back for one more long pull on the straw. She made a face as she swallowed.

He didn't even check the container, he simply handed it to Elaine, who removed it from the room. "All done! Way to go."

"Yay!" Carly clapped her hands. But then she dropped them to her sides and winced. "My tummy hurts."

"It's going to hurt," Dr. Searle said. "The special drink is taking all the green medicine out of your body. Pretty soon you're going to have to poop."

"Oh." Carly stared at him as if she'd never heard the word *poop* before.

Beth suppressed a smile. In Carly's world, doctors didn't use that word. Dr. Searle had said it with a straight face.

"And then the bad medicine will go right down the toilet and you can go home," he added.

"Hooray!" Carly said, then her face looked pained again. "My tummy hurts."

"It's going to hurt as the medicine works. Then you'll be all better. Listen—I have to check on my other patients. You watch your movie and tell your mommy when you have to go to the bathroom."

He looked at Beth for a moment and she felt herself flush under his brief appraisal.

"Press the call button when she needs the bathroom."

"Okay," Beth said.

His white coat snapped as he left the room.

"I'm sorry, Mommy," Carly said.

Since the retaining rails were not raised, Beth sat down on the bed next to her daughter. She gathered Carly into her arms. "It's okay," she told her simply. "I love you, and I forgive you. I'm just happy you're going to be okay."

"I'll never leave you. Not like Daddy," Carly said. She looked close to tears. "It hurts, Mommy."

"I know." Beth wished she could speed up the process. She stroked Carly's hair. "You'll never take medicine again without asking, will you?"

"No," Carly said. Under Beth's soothing ministrations, her daughter shook her head.

"I love you." Beth said as she drew Carly even closer. "I never want to lose you."

"You won't. I promise," Carly told her.

Beth leaned her daughter onto her back and kissed her forehead. "Good."

QUINTON STARED at the touching scene through the glass wall of Carly's room. Since no one had bothered to draw the privacy curtain, he had a perfect view.

"Carly freely admitted taking the medicine," Elaine said.

Quinton nodded. Whereas Beth Johnson was guilty of being irresponsible with her purse, she wasn't guilty of any type of child abuse. During his residency, he'd seen it all, including the mother who'd deliberately overmedicated her child, causing massive ulcers in her daughter's stomach lining that had eventually started to bleed. The child hadn't even been two.

No, Beth Johnson had made a mistake, and she was a far cry from a Division of Family Services case. He could sum up a person's character in a heartbeat, and he knew without a doubt that she was devoted to her child. She'd confirmed it in the conference room with her passionate plea for his understanding. He frowned, remembering. He hadn't liked his reaction to her.

He stared at the ink pen he held, which was emblazoned with some drug manufacturer's logo. Maybe tonight he was simply caving in from all the family pressure he was under. Perhaps he was still a tad burnt out from the holidays. He watched as Beth helped her daughter sit up. Beth Johnson was a natural nurturer. It was as if she'd never lost that proverbial glow from pregnancy that he saw on women's faces when they interviewed for their unborn child's future pediatrician. But Beth Johnson was somehow different, somehow more. He couldn't put his finger on it. Suddenly, the call button flashed and Elaine was on a run. Within moments, all three women had rushed to the bathroom.

Quinton sighed. That meant one thing: soon he'd be signing Carly's release papers and she and her hauntingly attractive mother would disappear into the night. They would fade into the faceless masses he treated when in the pediatric ER.

He turned and went to check on a new patient.

Chapter Two

"Come on, Quinton. Don't be such a fuddy-duddy. At least stay for the stripper."

Quinton lowered the half-empty bottle of beer. He *really* wanted to go home. Bachelor parties weren't exactly his thing, and worse, they reminded him, that, unlike most of the men in the room, he wasn't married. Not that Quinton was in a hurry to settle down and get married. That was what his family wanted him to do. But Quinton wanted the whole fantasy of love ever after, and was prepared to spend his life alone if he didn't find it. A man didn't marry because he was afraid of being alone. A man married because he'd found his perfect mate for life.

Unlike Bill, age forty-five. His bachelor party was for his second marriage. The first Mrs. Webber now enjoyed a house and a new BMW courtesy of her wealthy ex. The bride-to-be was twenty years younger than Bill. No, that type of relationship wasn't for Quinton.

He wanted a woman who loved him for him. He wanted the whole heart and soul, for better or worse, for richer or poorer, death-do-us-part thing. He wanted the fairy tale. Hell, he wanted what, in reality, probably didn't exist.

Quinton twisted the bottle in his hand. Maybe he shouldn't have been a doctor, especially one with ER duty. Doctors experienced too much negative reality. Jaded, Quinton knew the fairy tale was fake.

Unlike Carly Johnson. At four years of age, she had confused him for a prince. He was no prince. Quinton shook his head. Eight days had passed since Carly left the ER, and her small face still haunted him. She'd been pale but undeniably brave after her body had begun to purge itself of the liquid charcoal.

She'd even hugged him as she left, her small arms finding and tugging at the heartstrings he kept safely hidden. At that moment he'd looked into Beth Johnson's blue eyes and seen tears. Not tears of happiness, but of something else he hadn't been able to catch before she'd lowered her lashes and hidden the emotions. Images of Beth had haunted him, too, and that had never happened before. They remained as fresh as on the day they met—

"She's here," Larry said, interrupting Quinton's thoughts. "At least stay for this. Bill won't understand if you walk out early."

"Fine." Quinton tossed the empty bottle into a trash can. He could use the time to sober up a bit. Although he'd only had two beers, he rarely imbibed any alcohol, and he could definitely feel its effects. Besides, even though he disliked strip shows, maybe the tawdriness of it would help dispel his memories of the Johnsons. Quinton followed Larry into the family room and both men took a seat on the sofa.

"Everyone here?" Mike, one of the senior doctors in the practice, glanced around the room. "Great. Well, Bill, this little show's just for you, to give you a hint what you're giving up by being dumb enough to tie the knot again!"

Hooting and hollering followed as a woman entered the room. The large-brimmed hat she wore shadowed her face, and a tan trench coat covered her body. She set a boom box down, pressed a button and the music began. Catcalls resounded as she rotated her hips sensually. At the same time, she began to peel off her gloves, then tossed one of them over the head of the guy nearest to her. He responded with a loud whistle.

Quinton reached forward and, from the dish on the coffee table, grabbed a handful of peanuts. He should have left. He just hated these displays, they always embarrassed him. His highly moralistic mother had ingrained in him a sense of gentlemanly dignity and appreciation of a lady. Thus, he'd never been able to understand how a woman could sell her body to make money.

Deciding to take a clinical approach to the stripper, Quinton leaned back against the sofa and studied her as he had those pornographic films years ago during a six-hour-straight pornographic films desensitization exercise in med school.

Her hat still hid part of her face, but the trench coat

had been loosened to reveal her black lace outfit underneath. She did a maneuver in which she dropped to sit without a chair, and Bill grinned widely. The beer Quinton had had suddenly tasted old and pasty in his mouth. She stood up, flashed the crowd by opening and closing her trench coat, then simply opened the coat and let slip off her shoulders.

The words to the song were something about leaving the hat on but she tilted it up and away from her face. Once she turned around Quinton would be able to see her. But she arched her back and pivoted.

The trench coat fell to her feet and all the men except for Quinton hollered. Instead, he swallowed. Despite his clinical aloofness, the body underneath the black lace outfit appealed to him. The woman didn't have a perfect body, but her warm full curves made his fingers itch to touch them. She unhooked a garter belt and Quinton felt himself strain against his jeans. She straightened, and with a flick of her wrist, she finally sent the hat flying. Dark blond hair tumbled from beneath the hat and spread over her shoulders. Then she turned.

And Quinton froze.

Those lips. That nose. Those blue eyes. They'd stayed with him for the past two weeks.

He was on his feet in a second, next to her in maybe one more. She began to loosen a strap. "Stop," he said. He placed a hand on her arm.

For her to register that he wasn't just some drunk frisking a feel took a moment. Beth swatted Quinton's hand away. "What are you doing?" She kept her voice low, so only he could hear.

"I'm getting you out of here." He couldn't believe the force behind his words. To hell with the boos from his friends and acquaintances. They were married or about to be. They didn't need a peep show, especially of her. Hell, most of them wouldn't remember her face five minutes after she left.

What kind of a mother was she, anyway? He could still picture Carly's innocent eyes.

"Cut it out, Quinton. Whatcha doing?" someone called.

He really didn't know, nor did he answer, but like a possessed man, he circled Beth's wrist with his fingers and dragged her toward the kitchen.

"Let go of me," Beth said as she wrenched herself away. "I don't appreciate what you think you're doing. I have to finish my job—"

At that moment she recognized him. "Oh."

"'Oh' is right. Your job's finished."

"Quinton?" Larry poked his head around the cabinets. "Is everything okay?"

"Move on to the porno flicks or something. She won't be finishing. And bring me her stuff, will ya?"

"What do I tell Bill?"

"Make something up."

"You can't do this," Beth said.

"I just did," Quinton said, as Larry returned with Beth's things. "You had me so fooled." He shook his head savagely as he tossed her trench coat at her. "Let's go."

"I'm not going anywhere until you tell me…"

She must have seen the look in his eyes, for she headed toward the door. After telling Larry to make his excuses, that he'd explain later, he was right on her heels.

"Where's your car?" he demanded as they exited the building, his gaze roving the street.

"I took the L," she said.

"Then get in mine," he said. One hand still on her arm, with his free hand he fumbled for the remote and unlocked his Mercedes. When he reached for the door handle, she pulled away.

"Stop this. I'm not going anywhere with you. You've screwed everything up! Don't you get it? I had a job to do and—"

"Job's over. I'm taking you home. You won't go back inside." He glared at her, and she glared right back.

She must have believed him, though, for she said, "I can get home by myself. I don't even remember your name."

"I'm Quinton Searle. You can call me Quinton." His jaw set in a stubborn line. "And I'm taking you home."

Her chin came up as she held her ground. "I can take care of myself. You are not my keeper. I got here, didn't I?"

More possessiveness swept over him, even surprising him. "That's irrelevant. I'll drive you. In that getup at this time of the night you won't even make it to the L station without being accosted."

"Isn't that what you're doing?" Her ice-blue eyes blazed, and Quinton felt something inside him stir.

Damn, but she did things to him. Exactly *what* he wasn't certain, but he'd never yanked a woman out of a party before, much less a stripper. "I'm not attacking you. I'm saving you."

"Yeah, right," she said, but to his relief she complied and got in the car.

His respite from her verbal attack lasted mere seconds.

"You do realize that you just cost me five hundred dollars."

Quinton gripped the leather steering wheel tighter. Was that all her display was worth? His boat slip at Belmont Harbor cost more. Her chest heaved and the coat parted slightly. Quinton forced himself to keep his eyes on the road.

"You shouldn't be stripping. You have a child. You have a moral example to set."

"Oh thank you for that lecture, Mr. Moral Majority. How dare you accuse me of being a bad parent!"

He hadn't thought so in the ER. There, her love and tenderness for her child had impressed him. Seeing this side to her tarnished that earlier image and he lashed out.

"In two weeks I've observed two examples of your unfit parenting! Your little girl gets into your purse and eats medicine, and then I find you at a bachelor party shucking your clothes. That's pretty cut-and-dried to me, lady."

"You're a jerk and I'd never be your lady! Hell, I wouldn't even want to be your sister."

"That's good. My sister's a lawyer and getting married to a banker in four weeks. I doubt Shelby's ever taken off her clothes before multiple men in her life."

"'Ye who are sinless toss the first stone,'" Beth said.

"I will," Quinton replied, then snapped, "Where do you live?"

She rattled off an address. His eyebrows rose and he glanced at her. "You must do well. Pretty high-end, isn't it?"

Bitterness etched her features. "So high-end they're converting to condos and tossing out all the trash like me. And thanks to your interference tonight, I won't have the money to afford a security deposit for something else."

"Maybe you should get a real job."

"Maybe you should mind your own business."

He should. He shouldn't care, but the objectivity he had cultivated his whole life had fled. "I did once already. I could have hotlined your daughter's drug ingestion. Gotten Social Services on your tail. Hell, if I'd known you stripped for a living I would have."

"I don't strip for a living. I have a job!"

"You have a real job?" Even he heard how sharp he sounded, but he couldn't contain himself. "So tell me about your real job. Convince me why I shouldn't call Social Services anyway."

"You double-standard…uh! You think you're so high and mighty being a doctor and all, and there you were at a bachelor party! How many drinks did you have? Maybe I should flag down a cop. Have you tested for DWI."

"You do that." The effects of alcohol had fled and Quinton knew he was well below the legal limit. He never even would have considered driving otherwise. To his satisfaction, she settled against the leather seat with a thump. "Didn't think so."

"I realized it would mean more time in your undesired presence." Her voice, although lowered in volume, still had an edge to it.

Despite himself, he grinned. "Touché."

He parked the car by the curb outside her apartment building, right next to a sign announcing that the building was ninety-percent sold. She hadn't been lying about it being converted to condos, pricey ones at that.

"I'll walk you up so that no one sees you. Your neighbors don't know of your occupation, do they?"

Beth's blue eyes flashed as she held her temper in check. "For the last time, I am not a stripper. This was a one-time job that a friend arranged. I would have received five hundred plus any tips or bonuses." Defeat filled her voice. "You've messed everything up."

She stormed ahead of him, and he noted that the outer door wasn't locked. Not a very secure building. He followed her up to the second floor, and when she began to open her apartment door, the neighboring one opened. An elderly lady stuck her head out.

"Hi, Beth. You're home early."

"Yes," Beth said. She kept her back to Quinton as she spoke to the woman.

"Well, Carly's fast asleep. Why don't you just leave her until morning? Oh. That annoying Mr. Anderson came by tonight and dropped an official-looking letter under your door."

"Great." Beth threw her hands up into the air. "I asked him for more time, at least until the end of the month. Obviously not."

The neighbor looked sympathetic. "I told you that I'd store your stuff for you and that you can stay with me for a while. I told you I'd help you out any way I can."

"No. That's really sweet of you, but I can't. Really."

"Beth…"

"How about we talk about this tomorrow, when I get Carly?" Beth glanced at Quinton, and the elderly lady's eyes radiated understanding.

"Okay, dear." The woman closed her door.

As Beth opened her front door, Quinton glimpsed an envelope on the floor. As she stooped to grab it, impulse made him lean forward and snatch it first.

"Give me that!"

He held it up out of her reach. "I will when you tell me what's in it. The papers your neighbor mentioned?"

"Of course you would be the type to listen to other people's conversations. Yes, as a matter of fact, they're my eviction papers. Now, you've done more than enough tonight. Hand me that and go away. *Please.*"

She held out her hand and Quinton reluctantly placed the envelope in her outstretched fingers. She pressed it to her chest as if afraid he might change his mind.

"How long do you have?" he asked.

"None of your business," she snapped.

"How long?"

She shifted her weight to the other foot. "By noon Tuesday."

Could a landlord do that? "That's only three more days."

"Impressive. You can do math and yes, this is my *final* notice. He's been extending when I have to leave. I guess he just got tired of helping me this time." Beth tapped her foot impatiently. "Now that your curiosity is satisfied, just go."

As she stepped inside the apartment, Quinton had a raw need to make everything better somehow. He shook his head vigorously. She was not his charity case. She'd been stripping at a bachelor party, for goodness' sake!

"Good night," she said.

And with that, she shut the door firmly in his face.

Quinton stared at the closed door. Was she peering through the peephole to see if he was still there? He turned and walked away. Once, as his foot hit the step before the lower landing, he paused and thought about going back up. But what he would say or do when he banged on her door? Apologize? For what? Interfering? No, the best thing for him to do was to walk out of Beth's life and regain his detached professionalism and leave her an aberration of his past.

"ARE YOU SURE you don't have anything?" Beth demanded.

The woman behind the desk smiled sympathetically. "Not for a mother and a small child. Try the Adams Center down the street. Being the start of winter, we're full, but I've placed you on the waiting list. You're number three."

Beth stood and began the five-block walk back toward Luie's Deli. Number three on the waiting list wasn't good enough; she needed to be number one. And she'd already tried other shelters, but because Chicago had just had its first real cold snap, everything was full. Some new year she was having. Tomorrow Mr. Anderson would change the locks and anything left in the apartment would be tossed out with the garbage.

One month's rent was enough to avoid going to the shelter, and she had that saved. But without the security deposit, she'd had to pass on the apartment she'd found. Damn that interfering Dr. Quinton Searle!

"Hey, Beth." Nancy, Beth's boss, glanced up as Beth returned to the deli. "Laney just called. She's caught in construction traffic around Midway and can't make it back in time. I need you to deliver this for me."

"Sure." Beth didn't even shed her trench coat. She simply picked up the box of food. The aroma of the garlic bread drifted up to her nostrils. Although she'd just been on her lunch break, she hadn't eaten. "Where to?"

"The doctors' medical building. Right by the hospital. Lunch for the office staff or something. The address and suite number are on the order. Take the car. When you get back you can start on the pies."

"Okay." Beth accepted the keys Nancy handed her. The pies that Beth was to bake for tomorrow's event could wait an hour. Serving hot food was much more important.

She found the medical building easily; it was across from the hospital where she'd had the misfortune of meeting the seemingly illustrious Dr. Quinton Searle. Any pediatrician could have prescribed liquid charcoal, why had fate insisted she meet him?

Beth double-parked the car, left the flashers on and entered the building. Chicago Pediatrics had its offices on the seventh floor, and the box seemed to grow in weight as the elevator kept stopping to load and unload passengers at every floor. Finally, she stepped out of the elevator to find a solid mahogany door surrounded by beveled glass windows on each side marking the entrance to suite 712. She pushed open the door and walked up to the reception window. When she tapped, the glass slid back.

"Delivery from Luie's Deli."

The immaculate young brunette behind the desk brightened. "Great. Bring it in, will you?"

The large box containing many bags of food was now a lead weight.

The brunette pointed. "At the end of the hall and to the right you'll find the staff kitchen. The food is paid for, isn't it?"

Beth juggled the box so that she could check the ticket. "Yes."

"Great. Then just set it on the counter. There's an exit door to the left of the kitchen. You can go out that way."

"Thanks." On her trek down the long corridor she passed a few open rooms and noted others remained closed, the charts in plastic boxes and the colored metal flaps above the doors indicating patient status. The door to the last office she was about to pass was partially open.

"Libby will be right in to administer the shot. Be sure to call if there's any reaction. I'll see you for the six-month checkup."

Beth froze. No. It couldn't be. But walking out of the patient room was none other than Dr. Quinton Searle.

For a moment Beth looked furtively around, wishing that she could just dart into a patient room and hide for a few minutes. A nurse appeared and Quinton turned away from Beth before he saw her. Beth shifted her heavy box, mumbled an "Excuse me" and passed behind Quinton's backside.

Within seconds she'd located the kitchen and deposited the box. She took a moment to stretch her tired arms.

With a deep breath she made for the hallway, but suddenly a large white object filled the doorway.

"I THOUGHT THAT was your voice." Quinton stared at Beth. He felt his brow furrow. Had she become thinner since he'd last seen her? "What are you doing here?" Mentally he kicked himself. That had sounded dumb, which her answer "—Delivering food—" confirmed. She drew her chin up defiantly. He ignored it. "Your real job is delivering food?"

"Gee, I come in here with a box of food. What would you think? No strip show opportunities here. Now, if you don't mind, I have to get back. The car's double-parked."

"Is the food paid for?" He was reaching under his coat for his wallet.

She tried to inch by him and stopped. "It's paid for. I have to go."

"Don't we need to tip you?"

"Not unless you're giving me the five hundred dollars you cost me Saturday night." Beth marched forward, this time more determined to get through. "Now, I must leave. As I'll already be homeless tomorrow because of your meddling, the last thing I need to do is lose my job on top of everything else. Besides delivering food I bake pies and cakes, and I'm way behind schedule. So please…" She gestured toward the door.

Quinton stepped aside and let her pass. A moment later she was gone, once again having walked out of his life.

The office manager approached. "Who was that?"

"Your food's here."

His office manager cocked her head. "Oh. She's not the usual delivery girl."

So Beth didn't deliver food? Maybe she did bake. And had she said she'd be homeless tomorrow? A gnawing began in Quinton's stomach as he remembered the eviction papers.

"Tell me, where did you order from?"

"Luie's Deli. Canal Street."

"Great," Quinton said. He started for the exit. He

had a break between patients and if he hurried he could catch her and—

"Dr. Searle."

"Yes?" He turned back around. A receptionist stood there.

"Your mother's on line three. Says it's urgent."

"Thank you," Quinton said. His errand would have to be delayed. Mrs. Quinton Frederick Searle III—or Babs, to her friends—always indicated urgency whenever she called. Being a doctor's wife herself, she was a pro at working the system.

Quinton knew that the only urgency his mother had was to see him wed.

In his office he picked up the phone. "Mom," he said by way of greeting.

"Quinton! I was worried you were too busy."

"I'm on my lunch break."

"I'm not keeping you from eating, am I?"

Not unless she got long-winded. "No, I have a few minutes."

The requisite sigh. "Oh, good. You do remember Shelby and I will be there this weekend, don't you?"

"Yes."

"Super. We have some shopping to do. Unfortunately, Susannah won't be able to make it. You have asked her to wedding, haven't you?"

Susannah Joelle Phelps was his family's handpicked wife candidate for him. Twelve years younger than he was, Susie was twenty-three and in the throes of seeing all her best friends marrying. "No, I haven't."

"Quinton, please tell me you're not being rude to Susie. She's been waiting for you forever, and you're getting old son, old."

"I'm thirty-five, Mother, not dead. And don't worry, I've sent my tux measurements already."

"You better have. The wedding is Valentine's Day weekend. Don't even tell me that you didn't schedule off the week between your father's and my anniversary and your sister's wedding."

Quinton kept silent.

"You must be here, Quinton. There are family activities all week and you know your father really wants to talk to you. It's past time to return home. He's waited long enough, and, well, *I've* waited long enough. Once your sister is married the next thing on my agenda is organizing your wedding. I just want you happy. Susie and St. Louis would make a good combination."

"I'm happy here, Mother. And no, with Bill on his honeymoon I can't get away that week. I've already got people covering for me two weekends in a row."

"Stop hiding away from your family responsibilities. You have obligations. You are a Searle. Have I not raised you right?"

Uh-oh. Here came the lecture. "Mom, my nurse just told me I have ten calls to return. We'll talk soon."

"You need to be in the week before the wedding."

"I doubt that will happen."

"We'll talk this weekend. With my heart condition you know I can't take this kind of stress." Babs Searle definitely knew how to work the system. She'd always been over the top, a one-woman steamroller. But his father had asked Quinton to go easy on Babs because of her heart condition. And Quinton, although he had no desire to take over his father's practice, did love and respect his father.

Thus, the words were out of his mouth before he could even think to stop them. "By the way, I'm bringing a date to the wedding."

"What?" Silence fell as both Quinton and his mother contemplated what he'd just said. "Did I hear you correctly?" his mother finally asked.

Well, in for a penny…" Yes," Quinton said. "A date. But don't get your hopes up."

"So you aren't serious?"

"Mom, I'm never going to be serious about Susie, either. Stop stringing the poor girl along. Just because all her friends are getting married doesn't mean she'll be an old maid. You and her mother can matchmake somewhere else."

"Humph." His mother exhaled. "I'm not sure I—"

"Got to go, Mom," and with that Quinton hung up before she could get in another word.

He looked up to see Larry standing in the doorway.

"You have a date for your sister's wedding?"

"No," Quinton admitted. "But I have to do something or she'll book the chapel and have the bride waiting the minute Shelby's on her honeymoon."

Larry grinned. "I still think I have my old black book somewhere if you want."

"No, thanks," Quinton said. An idea started forming in his head. He'd cost Beth Johnson five hundred dollars. Well, he had a way for her to earn it back and not have to shuck her clothes in the process. As she was the most inappropriate woman for his parents' social circle he'd ever met, she'd be perfect for the job. He gave Larry a grin. "Believe me, I've got someone in mind who will get my mother off my back and not hassle me for a commitment afterward."

"Those are the best kind," Larry said.

WHEN QUINTON REACHED Luie's that evening at six, the woman behind the counter told him that Beth had gone for the day. Quinton purchased a slice of chocolate cream pie anyway, and ate it before returning to his car. The pie had been sinful, and Quinton resolved to do sixty push-ups, ten more than usual, when he got home that night.

The drive from Luie's to Beth's building took approximately twenty minutes in traffic—walking the short distance would have been quicker. Again, someone had left the door unlocked, saving him from having to be buzzed in. He took the steps two at a time to her floor.

Nervousness suddenly filled him as he inhaled a deep breath and knocked.

"It's open, Ida," he heard Beth call.

Quinton turned the knob and entered.

The sparseness of the place instantly appalled him. She really was moving; she hadn't been lying or exaggerating when she'd said she was being evicted. Boxes of stuff lined the walls, and faded rectangles of paint showed where pictures had once hung.

The apartment was tiny, probably one of the smaller units in the building. However the main room faced east, giving him a view of the Loop off in the distance.

"Ida, I've got most of everything—" Beth wiped her hands on her jeans as she came into the room. Her eyes widened and her mouth dropped open when she saw him. She froze. "What are *you* doing here?"

"Auntie Ida?" Running at full speed, Carly almost knocked Beth over.

Carly managed to dodge her mother, and before Quinton could move forward to steady Beth, Carly had tossed her arms around his legs and had given him a huge hug. "Dr. Searle!"

"Are you all right?" Quinton asked Beth as she steadied herself.

"What are you doing here?" she repeated.

"Checking up on me!" Carly blurted. She hadn't released her hold on his legs and her baby blue eyes gazed lovingly at Quinton. "I haven't taken any more medicine, and we're moving."

"I can see that. Your mommy told me about it."

"And I was serious," she said.

"I know that now," Quinton said. "Will an apology help?" Her expression told him no. "Where are you going?"

"A special place," Carly interrupted. "It's a surprise."

Quinton reached down and gently detached Carly's

arms from his legs. "I bet it is a surprise. Are you all packed?"

"Almost. Everything is going into boxes except for some of my clothes. And my blankie. Those go in a suitcase."

Quinton straightened and looked at Beth. She was staring at her child, and the pain in her eyes seared his heart. He'd caused this. She hadn't been lying. He understood, what Carly didn't—that her mother had no place to stay.

"What number are you?"

"Three at one place, six at another. But…" Beth pointed at Carly.

"I understand." Little ears did not need to hear. "Is there someplace we can talk?"

"Here I am." At that moment Ida appeared, and Beth was never so grateful to see her. "You've made some good progress. The movers will arrive at seven and I'll supervise while you're at work. You'll be all gone by Mr. Anderson's deadline." Ida paused as she saw Quinton.

Beth wanted to groan at the speculation she saw in her elderly neighbor's eyes.

"This is Dr. Searle," Beth offered.

"He saved me from dying at the hospital," Carly added.

"Well, I…" Quinton began.

"We met the other night but weren't formally introduced. I'm Ida Caruthers." She extended her hand and Quinton shook it. "It's nice to meet you. Are you here to help Beth pack?"

"He's here—he's…" Beth found herself oddly relieved when Quinton simply took charge and said, "Ida, would you mind giving us a few moments alone?"

"Certainly. Come on, Carly. I have some ice cream in my freezer and I can't eat it all."

"Do you have sprinkles?" Carly asked.

"Oh, I'll have to see what I can muster up. I may not have sprinkles, but I bet I have chocolate sauce."

"Yum," Carly said.

Moments later Beth found herself alone with Quinton.

"I'm sorry," he said.

"Don't be." She was too tired for anger, too tired for anything but bittersweet regret. "I fought the good fight, but no one wins against fate."

"Maybe you can."

"No, I can't. As of noon tomorrow I have to be out of here. I broke down and used the last of my money for movers and a storage facility. How I'll ever scrape up enough for a security deposit *and* first month's rent on a new apartment I don't know."

He'd caused this, and his conscience demanded he fix it. "Let me help."

"You can't."

Sure he could. He could solve any problem he set his mind to, except perhaps with his family. "Let me pay your security deposit for a new apartment. I'll even pay the first month's rent. You can pay me back whenever."

"I don't take charity."

"It's not charity. Consider it a loan. A favor. In fact, you can repay me with one."

Beth shook her head. "I won't take loans. Not from individuals. They end up being charity. And I dislike favors. They have to be repaid at too high a cost."

"Yet you'd strip to earn the money."

"Stripping was work. Not politically correct, but honest. I'm not a hooker and I don't strip bare. I've only done it a few times—a long time ago. It's quick money. I *needed* that money. But I waited too long— I didn't think Mr. Anderson would really evict me, not after the past few years I've had." She swallowed.

She was so tired, so sick of fighting to eke out an existence. Still, she pressed on. "You wouldn't know what it's like to be poor, would you? You wouldn't know how hard it is to put food on the table, to make sure your child doesn't suffer. You wouldn't know…" She suddenly saw two of Quinton.

Both Quinton's spoke. "Beth, you don't look good. You're pale and…"

"I'm fine," Beth said. "I'm just fine." She was always fine. She couldn't afford not to be.

And then, as if fate mocked her, the world went black.

Chapter Three

When she awoke, it was to gentle light and a pillow underneath her head. Where was she? Panic filled her and Beth forced herself to try to sit. Pain filled her head.

"Relax." Quinton's voice. "You need to rest."

Beth closed her eyes and let herself sink back into the softness. Then she remembered.

"Carly." Beth's frantic voice came out a mere whisper.

"She's fine. Ida's got her." Quinton's voice was reassuring. "Just rest," he said again. "Carly's fine. Right now she's probably watching *Mulan*."

She kept her eyes closed. "Why are you still here?"

"Because you passed out in my arms. When's the last time you had something to eat?"

"I don't remember. Maybe lunch?"

"Which was hours ago."

Beth's eyelids snapped open, the light was too intense. She closed her eyes, waited a moment and tried again. Although this time her eyes adjusted better, she still winced. She then struggled to sit up.

"Not so fast," Quinton said. "Let me help you."

She felt his arms around her as he moved her to a sitting position.

One arm around her, he said, "Now that you're up, drink this." With his other hand, he brought a cup to her lips.

Parched, Beth allowed herself a long drink of the grape-flavored liquid. It tasted familiar. "What is it?"

"Sports drink. Full of electrolytes. I drink it after I work out. I had a bottle in my car. In my medical opinion, your body is dehydrated, hungry and plain fatigued. You need rest and hydration."

Beth struggled to free herself from his arm. "I'm fine. I have a lot to do, and you need to go."

A firm but gentle hand on her shoulder stopped her from rising.

"You're not fine. You collapsed and lost consciousness."

"I—" Beth began.

"No excuses, no protests. I'm a doctor, and if you want a second opinion regarding your physical condition I'd be happy to take you to the ER. Northwestern is right around the corner and I have some good friends there who would be happy to check you out, maybe even give you an IV."

Quinton removed his arm and Beth let the soft pillow claim her head. No more ER visits—ever. Besides, she certainly didn't have the money for another fifty dollars' co-pay. "That's okay. I'm not that bad off."

"See, I knew you were a wise woman," Quinton

said. "Now, you're going to stay right here and drink the rest of this. You've let yourself get run-down. If you were twenty years younger, I'd insist you go to a hospital."

"Really, I'm fine."

"You have to rehydrate. Let me help you." He cradled her head and supported it while Beth took another swallow of the milk.

"And then I'm getting off my couch."

"No, you're not," Quinton said easily.

Beth sipped the grape-flavored sports drink until the cup was empty. Then he lowered her back to the pillow.

"That's better."

Beth gazed up at him. "I have to finish packing."

Quinton ignored her. "Now that you're done this, I'm going to get you some more. We'll talk about your activities after that."

Despite herself, Beth cracked a small smile. "Yes, Doctor."

The smile Quinton gave her in return before he stood could have melted even the hardest of hearts. Beth found her own fluttering.

"That's my girl," he said.

I wish! Beth's hand shook as she adjusted the ratty old blanket he'd covered her with. Had she really just thought that? She stared at the flat brown doors of her apartment. Then she glanced at the clock.

Panic overtook her. She had things to pack! Stuff to move! She couldn't relax for another moment.

"I told you to remain lying down." Quinton's voice cut through the room.

Beth paused, her left foot halfway to the floor. "I have to pack the rest of my things. I have to be out by noon tomorrow and—"

"It'll all to be taken care of. I've hired packers."

Disbelief filled her as she stared at him. Was he serious? His gray eyes indicated that he was. But how? Quinton set a tray down and ran a finger under the collar of his long-sleeved polo shirt. "As I keep saying, you need to rest."

She had to concentrate on her priorities, her symptoms and Quinton's good looks notwithstanding. "My stuff. I have to pack my stuff."

He shrugged. "No, you don't. I said I took care of it. I called in a favor." He saw her expression and smiled. "Yeah, a favor. A friend of mine owns a moving service. Everything for storage goes at first light tomorrow, and he's got a two-man crew coming to box your personal things at the same time."

"But I have no place to go!"

"Trust me." Quinton opened another bottle of the drink that he'd brought up from his car. "Carly deserves a mother who's well."

Anger returned, and Beth winced as her head throbbed harder. "I am not one of your patients! You can't order me about. I'm not drinking anything until you tell me exactly what's happening. I can't afford this."

"Stop stressing yourself out. It's not good for you. I can afford it."

"But I can't. I told you before—I'm not taking your charity or your favors!" Beth sat up completely, the blanket slipping to her waist. She glanced down in a panic.

"Don't worry," Quinton said. "You're decent. Besides, I saw it all the other night."

Beth shot him a dirty look. "If I drink this stuff, will you tell me what you want and then leave?"

"I want to help you." He handed her the bottle of sports drink.

"What's in it for you?"

Quinton frowned. "Am I that transparent?"

"Men always want something," Beth said.

"That doesn't say much for my gender. And I guess, in a way, I do want something. But it's not what you're expecting. At least, I hope not. What I think is that I have a solution to your problem, and in turn, you can be the solution to mine."

"Wait. You're telling me that *you* have a problem you want *me* to solve. That's what you want? A solution to a problem?"

"What, you find it hard to believe that I have a problem? That's a bit low, don't you think?"

"I don't mean for it to be. It just appears that you have everything going for you." Beth thought for a moment. It was true that everyone had problems. There were health problems, relationship problems and money problems. Then there was… "You're not on drugs, are you?"

Quinton's head snapped backward and disbelief

caused his eyes to narrow. "No! What gave you that idea?"

Beth waved a hand. "I was trying to figure out what type of problem you have. You've obviously got money, you appear to be in great health and with your good looks you can't be lacking a girlfriend."

"You find me attractive?" A teasing note entered Quinton's voice, as he tried to lighten what was fast becoming an awkward moment.

Beth's heart jumped, but outwardly she remained calm. "No. I said you were good-looking. That doesn't mean I'm attracted to you. Anyway, if you don't have those problems, maybe you're like one of those guys in the soaps who's the closet drug user."

"Uh, no," Quinton said. "Not even close, and I'm a bit offended that you thought that of me. Now, drink."

"I'm sorry I keep offending you. I'm not trying to." Beth took a drink. "Okay, so then what is it?"

"My parents want me to return to St. Louis to live."

The drink almost fell from Beth's hand, but she caught it before it spilled. "That's all?"

This time Quinton really appeared offended. "That's all you have to say?"

"Oh, come on. You're not dying. You're not being evicted. You're not on drugs. Your parents just want you to move to St. Louis, where I assume they live and you grew up. So you say no. No big deal. How hard is it to say no? You're a big boy."

"Yes, I am. But unfortunately, simply saying no to what you've been groomed to do since birth is a little awkward. It is a big deal. While my problem may not seem big to you, it is to me."

Beth set down the sports bottle. He was correct and she was being totally insensitive. She normally wasn't like this. Maybe she was feeling the stress of everything, but that was no excuse for her behavior. She'd simply dismissed his problem. The very least she could do was to hear him out. After all, he had rescued her when she fainted.

"I'm sorry. I usually don't jump to conclusions. You've also been very kind to me. It's the least I can do. Why don't you tell me about it?"

Quinton took a deep breath. "I've been raised since birth to take over my father's pediatrics practice, marry, join the country club and live in a nice part of town. While I love pediatric medicine, I don't love the girl my parents want me to marry and I have no desire to live in either Ladue or Town and Country. And then there's my mother. She's as upper crust as they come and my father is very patriarchal. I'm the eldest child, and besides passing my name to my son, I'm to carry on the family traditions, just like he did. It's my birthright and my responsibility."

"So, you have to make them understand that times change. You've chosen a different path."

"It's not that easy," Quinton said. "They can't accept thirty-five, single and happy in Chicago. They see bachelorhood as some sort of failure—not as a lifestyle choice. They've even arranged for a date to my sister's wedding which is four weekends from now, on February twelfth."

"An arranged date? They still do those things?"

"My mother's idea. It will be an arranged marriage if she has her way. Shelby's wedding is almost here, and afterward my mother will have an emotional let-down and nothing to do. She'll turn to me. Actually, she's already started." Quinton took a deep breath. "So I told my mother I was bringing a date. Which is why I came over here tonight."

"I don't see how I can help you with any of this. I don't have any experience in this area. I'm not from a wealthy family. My parents are divorced and live on opposite coasts. I hardly see them. We're not what you call close. I don't understand these family matters."

"That doesn't matter." Quinton suddenly seemed impatient. "Let me just be blunt. Here's my idea. I want you to be my date in exchange for a place to live."

"You *what?*"

"I want you to pretend to be madly in love with me and go to the wedding with me."

He stared at her and she stared back. He opened his mouth to offer her five hundred dollars, but another idea popped into his head. Beth Johnson needed more than five hundred. She needed time to get well and get back on her feet. She needed a chance. He'd screwed things up for her—she was right about that—and he had to make amends.

"Move in with me for a month or so," he continued. "Just long enough to let you and Carly get back on your feet. You'll have your own two rooms. With my hours

I'm never home, and no one will think anything of me picking up some extra ER shifts to give you privacy. Plus, the weekend of February fifth, I'll be in St. Louis for my parents' anniversary. The weekend after that is the weekend I want you to go with me to my sister's wedding in St. Louis and pretend to be my date."

"You're crazy." Beth gazed at him to make sure she'd actually heard what she thought she had. His expression indicated he was serious. "You're asking me to live with you and pretend to be in love with you at a wedding? This is insane."

Quinton nodded. "Probably, but it'll work. It's less messy than finding a wife and it'll keep my family off my back. It'll provide you a place to live and some time to save up your security deposit. We each get what we want. And don't think you can't do it—I know you can. You're a beautiful woman. All we have to do is get you gussied up and my family should be satisfied that I'm happy. You just keep insisting that you could never leave Chicago. Hopefully, they'll relent and give up asking me to leave once you're in the picture. Afterward you'll dump me and I'll remain heartbroken for at least a year."

He'd said she was beautiful, and she'd liked it. She mentally shook her herself. "But wouldn't they want you to change cities after your breakup so you could leave the memories behind? They'll probably also start really throwing women at you, to help you get over me."

He frowned. "Hmm. I hadn't thought of that. Maybe

I'll tell my parents that we have a chance of working things out. That might buy me some more time until I can figure out what to do. Maybe you should be my fiancée and not just my date."

Quinton's fiancée. The idea sounded so seductive. Beth fought the devil whispering over her shoulder. "I don't know why this is necessary. You could simply say no."

He stood up and paced. "I've done that more than a dozen times, but to no avail. My family won't accept my choices. Besides, my mother has a heart condition. As a doctor, I know it's not as serious as she maintains, but it's real. My dad asked me not to upset her. Believe me, I'd rather tell my mother the truth but I promised. If lying about our relationship means adding a few extra years to her life, I will. Despite her flaws, she's my mother."

Beth knew all too well about extra years. Randy hadn't had any. But then, Quinton's family could afford top medical treatment. Randy couldn't.

"Castles in the air collapse," Beth warned.

"I realize all the pitfalls," Quinton said. "I understand honesty is the best policy and all that. I made my intentions about my career clear to my family from the start. But what do you do when the other party refuses to listen, refuses to consider your wishes? What do you do then?"

He did have a point. "I'm not sure."

"Exactly. That's the situation I'm in, which is why I'm asking for your help. You get free room and board, some new clothes and some time to start over, and I get freedom from my well-meaning but misguided mother, who has my doting father wrapped around her little finger."

"You could just give me the money from my lost job."

Quinton smiled, but the mirth didn't reach his deep gray eyes. "That is not an option I'm considering." *At least, not any longer.* No, he liked this new idea much better.

"Figures."

Somehow she had finished the second sports drink, and Quinton took it from her and began to retreat toward the doorway. "I'm going to throw this away and check on Carly. I'm sure she wants to see you, and you her."

"Oh, yes," Beth said.

"Think about my idea while I'm gone. It would suit both of us." With that, he left the room and closed the door behind him.

Once again Beth found herself staring at the door. Quinton had been so attentive, so caring. But then, he'd had an ulterior motive. He needed her to pretend to be his fiancée.

The thought thrilled her, and at the same time repulsed. After all, what a joke. She knew why she was the perfect candidate for the job. She wasn't rich, she was child-challenged and she certainly didn't fit in with the college-degreed medical set. She was ordinary, the girl from the proverbial wrong side of the tracks. A man like Dr. Quinton Searle would never date, much less marry, a woman like her.

Then again, maybe if he got to know you, he might.

Beth tossed that fantasy aside as Carly, followed by Quinton, bounded into the room and clambered up onto the couch. Her pigtails bounced as she gave her mother a huge hug.

"Mommy, Auntie Ida and me been playing video games."

"Auntie Ida and I," Beth said automatically.

"Auntie Ida and I," Carly repeated. "It's so fun. And I saw some of *Mulan*. I have lots of games left to play."

Beth glanced up at Quinton. "Ida got a PlayStation?"

Quinton shrugged. "I have a PlayStation at my house."

"They're fun, Mommy," Carly said. "I want to go to Quinton's—"

"Dr. Searle," Beth corrected.

Carly's face puckered.

"I told her she could call me Quinton," he said.

Carly brightened. "See, Mommy. It's okay if I call him that. Quinton told me he has a big-screen TV. He said it's like those ones in the stores!"

Beth reached forward and ruffled Carly's blond hair. A kid in a candy store—that was her daughter. Could she let a little girl like this live in a shelter?

She glanced at Quinton. He could be the devil himself and she would accept his offer. She had no choice. Hopefully, he was an angel in disguise—although, given her experience, she doubted it. Angels didn't look after Beth Johnson.

And so, she acquiesced and allowed Quinton to load them into his car and take them to his apartment. Carly had left their tiny place without a second look, and once in Quinton's home, declared that she'd found heaven.

Once Quinton had settled Beth in a bedroom, he said, "Carly, your mommy still needs to rest. Why don't you go play another game?"

"Okay!" Carly leaned over and gave Beth a quick kiss. "I'm going to go play. I love you, Mommy."

Beth's heart broke and tears threatened as her daughter climbed off the bed and rushed out the bedroom door. The devil be damned.

"Are you okay?"

Beth turned her face away from his probing gaze. "Fine—" she mumbled, praying that he wouldn't notice the way her voice had cracked.

"Sure?"

Anger consumed her suddenly, and she turned back around. She'd gone to a twilight universe. The bedroom she was in had colonial trim, crown molding and chair rail. Some designer had painted it a robin's-egg blue. The comforter she clutched to her chest was white. White curtains were drawn back to display a floor-to-ceiling view of the night sky and the dark blue horizon of Lake Michigan. A clock on a cherry dresser revealed that it was almost nine p.m.

"No, I'm not sure. I collapsed, my stuff is in storage, I'm taking your charity and my daughter thinks she's found nirvana. What could possibly be wrong with this picture?"

"Beth."

She pounded her fist into the soft cover. "No. Quinton, I'm sorry, but I can't accept your offer. We'll leave tomorrow. Carly can't get accustomed to this lifestyle. We don't live like this. We'll never live like this." Beth gestured toward the windows and their magnificent view. "This isn't our world. If we stay in it, how will we get back to ours? I own ratty blankets, not expensive bedspreads. How do I go back?"

Quinton's face fell. "I'm not sure," he replied. "You're right. I'm sorry. I was insensitive. I never should have suggested this scheme. I was only thinking of myself."

"No, you aren't insensitive. You have a problem to solve, just as I do. I'm just not your solution. You can't take the easy way out of this one."

"You're right. But at least stay here until you get another place. Seriously. Take as long as you want. You aren't well, and if you don't rest up, you'll relapse. At least this way I'll know you'll be safe and not out on the street or in a shelter somewhere. You don't have anywhere to go, do you?"

"No more than a few days," Beth whispered. She hated him at that moment for pointing out the obvious. Not that she truly hated him, but he was an easy target. She hated that her life had spiraled so far out of control. She'd done everything, played by the rules.

This had to be rock bottom. It had to be. Her head throbbed and she winced. She'd worry about the money for a security deposit tomorrow.

"I'm tiring you." Quinton shook his head in disbelief, a black strand of hair falling into his face. He angrily pushed it back. "I'm a doctor. I know better. You need rest and some acetaminophen. I'm going to get you some. Plus, I'm sure it's past Carly's bedtime."

He paused, his hand on the doorknob. "You'll feel better in the morning and we can talk about this then. Just don't rush out, Beth. Make yourself well first. You owe your daughter that. You owe your daughter a healthy mother."

And Beth knew she did. Carly's father had died; Beth had to stay healthy. She nodded at Quinton.

"You'll stay?"

"I'll stay."

Relief covered his face. "Good. I'm sorry this happened to you, Beth. I really am. It's partly my fault, and for that I apologize. I know you don't believe me, but I am sorry. You tell me what you want me to do."

With that he walked out of the room, leaving Beth to stare at the white six-panel door. Her husband Randy had never apologized, never found any fault to be even one percent his. Carly had called Quinton a prince. His actions had shown him to be a knight. Perhaps he was a bit misguided, but all the qualities were there. Too bad he wasn't hers.

She was a damsel who would have to save herself.

THREE DAYS LATER Beth had recovered enough to find herself with Friday-afternoon cabin fever. Quinton had hired Jena, the nurse from the hospital. Jena had had some vacation time coming, and she'd jumped at the chance to earn extra cash. Beth didn't even want to consider what Quinton was paying Jena. Worse, he'd even wrangled from Luie's a week's paid vacation for Beth.

They never had talked. He'd check on her in the morning, say she needed more rest, then disappear for the majority of the day, presumably to his practice. As far as Beth could tell, he hadn't picked up any ER shifts, and thus had been home most evenings. She'd been coerced into staying in bed, while she assumed he entertained her daughter with video games and big-screen TV.

It was time for them to discuss the situation. She'd admitted to herself that it would be better to borrow his money than to accept his charity any longer. She had to get Carly away from this addictive life of wealth and privilege. She had to get herself away, as well, especially from Quinton.

The more she saw of him, even what little it was, the more she liked him. His gray eyes held concern for her. His lips would smile just so, and Beth would feel an indescribable tingle of happiness. Not only was he gorgeous, but he had the warm, caring and sensitive personality so many men lacked. Even after his proposition and her refusal, Quinton had remained a gentleman.

Beth wrapped her arms around herself. The apartment was warm and toasty; outside, the Chicago wind tossed Lake Michigan into whitecaps.

However, this wasn't her world. It never had been, and she couldn't let it draw her in and seduce her now.

Carly had taken to privilege like a fish to water— maybe she'd been born to it! Today she and Jena were at the Chicago Children's Museum, probably having the time of their lives. Beth expected them home any moment. Monday, she decided, she'd start finding someplace to live. Maybe they could be in their new apartment by Friday. Yes, it would be rough, but they'd managed before.

The doorbell sounded, and Beth frowned. Had Jena forgotten her key? Beth walked to the door and looked through the peephole. Two women stood there, immaculately groomed, in heavy fur coats. Even with the warped view through the peephole, Beth knew the fur was real, though she had no idea what kind of fur it was. The doorbell shrilled again.

"Quinton, open up," one of them demanded.

Not knowing what else to do, Beth unlocked the front door and peered out. "May I help you?"

Surprise was quickly replaced by appraisal. The elder of the two women spoke. "I'm looking for my son. His office said he was on his way home."

Beth grimaced. Perhaps she shouldn't have opened the door. The fragrance of expensive perfume wafting to her nose made Beth immediately aware of how horrid she must appear. It had been the first day she'd fully dressed, but she'd only pulled on old faded sweat clothes. Her hair, although clean, remained a fright and desperately needed a good stylist.

Beth stepped into the living room, and the two women followed.

"He is expecting us. I told him Monday when I phoned. How like him to forget. I'm Babs Searle, Quinton's mother." Gray eyes like her son's narrowed.

Beth swallowed.

"This is his sister, Shelby. And you are?"

Beth was saved from replying by the arrival of Jena and Carly.

"Mommy! You should have seen the dinosaur egg—" Carly stumbled over the word "—egshibit. And there was a tree house and I played in the water and…it was so fun!" Carly tossed herself into Beth's arms and gave her mother a kiss. Beth set her back down and Carly raced toward the kitchen. "Is Quinton home yet? I bought him a souvenir. It's in Jena's purse. I'm hungry."

"Let's go get some food," Jena offered, her wary expression saying she'd rather hide in the kitchen than figure out what was going on and who these people were.

Carly waited in the doorway. "Okay. Hot dogs? Can I have a hot dog?"

"*May* I have a hot dog," Beth automatically corrected.

"May I?" Carly asked.

It was Jena who answered. "Certainly you may have a hot dog, but you need a vegetable, as well. What do you want, carrots or green beans? Come with me and we'll figure it out."

As Carly and Jena disappeared into the kitchen, Beth wished she, too, could hide somewhere. Quinton's mother and sister were now openly staring at her, one woman in total fascination and the other in absolute disgust.

"You're living here?" his mother said, her disbelief obvious. "You're living with my son?"

A movement at the front door to the apartment caught Beth's peripheral vision and she turned her head. Quinton stood there, and from his weary expression she realized he'd heard his mother's cryptic words.

"Mother," he said. "What a pleasant surprise. Hi, Shelby."

"Hi," his sister said.

Babs Searle took off her gloves and slapped them into her palm. "Quinton, don't tell me you forgot we were coming to Chicago to shop? I told you we were. Is this your date to Shelby's wedding? And is this what it seems? She's living here? With her child?"

Quinton stepped into the apartment and began to close the door. Beth hadn't known him long, but he appeared to age, in that instant, well beyond his thirty-five years. Her decision, her instinctive need to protect the man who'd rescued her, came fierce. Before Quinton could respond to his mother, Beth found herself moving forward. Not caring that she wore old sweats, she stood up on her tiptoes and gave him a quick kiss on his lips.

The aftershocks of the kiss almost made her lose her concentration, but seeing the *O* of surprise on Quinton's mother's lips made Beth remember. She wrapped her arms around Quinton's waist, ignoring the sensations shooting through her body. *Adrenaline.* That was all this sudden fluttering inside her body was.

Quinton's arms tightened on hers, and Beth dared not raise her gaze to his. Instead, she focused on his mother and getting the words out with conviction.

"Mrs. Searle, it's a pleasure to finally meet you. Let me put your mind at ease. Why shouldn't I live here? I'm Beth, I love your son and he's asked me to marry him."

Chapter Four

Quinton tried to keep his jaw from hitting the ground. With his mother's gaze moving back and forth from Quinton to Beth, there was no way Quinton could let any part of his nonverbal body language reveal that Beth's announcement had floored him.

But shock him she had. Earlier this week, she'd said no to his scheme. Now she'd changed her mind and sprung it on him. But right now wasn't the time to ask Beth why. Right now she was pressed up against him, her hip connected with his, her arm laced around his waist.

His body liked it. A lot. His toes still tingled from her brief kiss. Part of him wanted nothing more than to ignore his mother, lift Beth up, carry her into the bedroom and explore these new sensations that were consuming his body. He wanted to taste her skin, feel her mouth on his again.

His mother's words sobered him like a cold shower. "Quinton? Is this true? You've asked her to marry you?"

"Uh, yeah." The words confirming his engagement

and his and Beth's arrangement managed to get past Quinton's lips. He pulled Beth around beside him so that her hand splayed across his chest. He had an intense desire to see her eyes. Instead, Beth clutched his shirtfront and buried her head in his chest. "Yes, I've asked Beth to marry me."

Quinton freed one of his hands and lifted Beth's chin. Ah, there were those blue eyes. They'd darkened with…Quinton didn't think what he saw there was fear. More like awareness…and uncertainty.

Quinton's lips curved into a smile. "She said yes, didn't you, darling?" Before Beth could say anything, Quinton lowered his lips to hers for another kiss.

He tasted the sweetness of her mouth immediately and a raw groan overtook him. He'd only meant the kiss to be an innocent one, but when Beth's lips parted, he deepened the kiss and her eyes closed. Her fingers relaxed. No longer was she clutching his shirt; rather, her fingers kneaded, trying to feel under the fabric. He shifted position.

"A-hem, well."

Quinton felt Beth stiffen as his mother's voice broke the moment.

"I can see you're obviously compatible in one way."

"I think it's wonderful," Shelby said. "My elder brother in love. Congratulations."

Quinton loosened his hold on Beth, but not enough that she could move away. He locked eyes with his mother. "We're very compatible," he said. "She fits me perfectly."

Which wasn't actually a lie. From that kiss, Quinton had learned that Beth Johnson did fit him. Her mouth had when he'd kissed her, and right now her body still curved perfectly into his. When they went to bed it would be…

"So, how did you meet?" Shelby asked.

Quinton stared at his sister. She smiled at him—the smile of one soon to be married, one who wants everyone else to be equally in love and happy.

"And can we sit down? My feet are killing me."

"Oh, I'm sorry. You've been shopping all day. Where are my manners?" Quinton gestured toward the sofas. "Please, sit. Can I get you anything? I have soda and water and—"

"We're fine," his mother interrupted. She took off her fur coat and draped it over an armchair as she settled onto a black leather sofa. "So tell me the whole story. Every single word. How did you two lovebirds meet?"

As soon as his mother asked the question, Beth panicked. She was way out of her league here. First off, Babs Searle was smart. Second, Beth knew she certainly wasn't the type of wife candidate Mrs. Searle would want for her son and that this conversation wouldn't be smooth. Third…Beth wasn't good at deception and she was already so muddled from Quinton's wonderful kiss that she couldn't *remember* her third point. That didn't bode well.

"We…" Beth began. Her gaze turned to catch Quinton's. He seemed to understand, for he touched a fingertip to her nose. The intimate movement made Beth's heart jump, allowed him to guide her to the sofa across from where his mother and sister sat.

"We met at the emergency room," Quinton said as they sat down. "Her daughter had an accident, and I was the doctor on call. We've been seeing each other ever since."

He'd told nothing but the truth, and somehow it had worked.

"Right," Beth said. Quinton settled an arm around her shoulders. The weight was oddly comforting. As was her decision to let him do all the talking.

"So, what do you do?" His mother clasped her hands in her lap and peered at Beth. Beth wanted to run a hand through her messy hair, but she remained still.

"Beth's a chef," Quinton said. "Specifically pastries. Cakes, pies, those things."

"I see," Babs said, her drawn-out emphasis on the second word indicating that she found the occupation deficient, definitely not good enough for a Searle.

Shelby, however, smiled and tried to find some common ground with Beth. "Too bad I didn't know that earlier, or you could have done my wedding cake."

"Lake Forest is doing your wedding cake," Babs said. "It's on Clayton Road."

Beth shrugged. Obviously Lake Forest was one of *the* bakeries in St. Louis, but that meant nothing to her. She'd never been there. Her mouth moved, defying her brain's command to stay closed. "I've lived in

Chicago all my life, sorry. I've never even left Illinois."

"Really." Babs's tone masked her disdain, but Beth knew it was there. "So how do you feel about St. Louis?"

She should have kept her mouth shut. "I'm sure it's a pretty city," Beth said.

Beth could see Babs mentally adding *not well traveled* to Beth's list of flaws.

"Well, you'll see it soon enough I'm sure. Certainly Quinton has told you he has plans to relocate to his hometown. He is slated to take over his father's successful medical practice."

With his free arm, Quinton reached over and began to toy with Beth's fingers. "That's not for certain, and yes, Beth and I have discussed it."

Babs's eyes narrowed. "Well." She seemed at a momentary loss for words. "So this was love at first sight?"

Quinton squeezed Beth's hand. His warmth strengthened her.

"Absolutely. She fell right into my arms."

Beth somehow kept a straight face. She had fallen, in a dead faint. But not from love. "Would you and Shelby like to stay for dinner? I'm sure I could whip up something."

"Oh, no." Babs shook her head. "Shelby and I have reservations. We'll tell the maître d' to make it for two instead of three, now that Quinton has forgotten about it. Besides, you don't look to going out."

"She's not," Quinton said. "Beth's had a bit of a cold."

"Oh," Babs said.

Beth wondered where on the list deficiency "unhealthy" ranked. "Well, we shouldn't take up any of your time. After all, we'll have all of next weekend to get to know each other." She stood and Shelby followed. "You are bringing her for the prewedding festivities, aren't you?"

Beth felt Quinton stiffen before he stood up.

"We haven't discussed it," he said. "As I said earlier, Beth's not been well."

His mother began to fan herself with her hand, and Beth remembered Mrs. Searle's heart condition. "Is it getting hot in here?" Babs asked.

Although Beth suspected that Babs Searle had probably learned to get her way by using her condition, Beth knew better than to chance aggravating the woman. And Beth *had* told Quinton that she would help him out with his family. She'd actually started this charade today. She couldn't back out now. She rose to her feet.

"Mrs. Searle, we'd be delighted to come," Beth said.

"Wonderful." Babs looked better already. "We'll expect you Thursday afternoon—since I assume you're driving?"

"Yes," Quinton said.

"And you are planning on staying at the house?" Babs's left eyebrow arched.

"Yes," Quinton said. "Carly can room with Beth."

"Not necessary," Babs said. "Carly can have the old

nursery. Although I must tell you both that I frown on premarital liaisons in my home."

"I have my own room here," Beth said.

"Here is probably too late, my dear. But at least you are getting married. Although—" She paused and stared at Beth's left hand for a moment. Her lips pursed in displeasure. "Where is her ring, Quinton?"

"Ring?" He appeared both surprised and shocked.

Babs pointed at Beth. "Yes. Her ring. Her engagement ring. Surely you are planning on putting a diamond on her finger."

"My ring is getting resized," Beth offered; after all, what was one more little white lie? "We picked it out a few days ago."

Quinton ran his fingers through the hair at her nape. The intimate gesture, probably only meant to fool his mother and to say thanks for covering, sent heat throughout Beth's body. Darn, but Dr. Quinton Seale certainly had a magical touch. It was doing the strangest, oddest things to her…

"We'll have her ring before next weekend," Quinton said, sounding more certain. "You'll see it then."

Carly bounded into the room at that moment. "Hey, Mom! I ate two hot dogs. Can I have some ice cream now?"

"Sure," Beth said, too flustered from the delicious sensations shooting through her body from Quinton's touch to correct Carly's grammar. Beth stepped out of Quinton's grasp and toward her daughter as Jena, an apologetic look on her face, came into the room.

"Great. I love ice cream," Carly said. "Two big scoops. Okay, Jena?" Carly paused a moment, as if sensing that the grown-ups had something big on their minds. "Whatcha all talking about?"

"Carly," Beth reproved. "You don't interrupt an adult—"

"We were discussing next weekend," Babs said. She stared at Carly as though contemplating something, rose and walked toward her. "How old are you?" Babs asked.

"I'm four," Carly announced. She held up and wiggled four fingers for emphasis.

"That's what I thought." Babs gave a dramatic sigh and turned toward her daughter. "Shelby, you do realize what this means? We'll have to get her a dress and a basket. It's totally inappropriate not to have her in the wedding party, given her age and the fact that she will be Quinton's stepdaughter. You'll just have to have two flower girls."

Shelby seemed used to Babs's decisions, and Beth wondered how many other wedding plans Quinton's mother had altered.

"That's fine," Shelby said. "I'm sure the boutique will have a dress her size. If not, they can special-order it."

"What size is she?" Babs asked, directing the question toward Beth this time.

A lump formed in Beth's throat, however, but she knew she had no choice but to answer. "She wears a five."

"Good. I'll order her a flower girl dress tomorrow." Babs began to put on her coat and Quinton rose and went to help her. "Thank you," she said to her son. "Carly can try on the dress when she's in St. Louis."

Carly suddenly pulled on Beth's arm, ice cream momentarily forgotten. "I'm getting a dress? A new dress? A special dress?"

Beth saw the excitement in her daughter's blue eyes. Carly hadn't had a new party dress in ages.

Babs was the one who responded. "Oh, yes. You're going to get a brand-new dress so that you can be a flower girl in your aunt Shelby's wedding. Before Aunt Shelby says her vows, you and Tara will walk down the aisle and cover it with flowers."

"I'm going to be in a wedding?" Carly clapped her hands and gazed hopefully up at her mother. Then she frowned, as if confused. "Who's Aunt Shelby?"

"I'm Shelby," Quinton's sister volunteered as she stood. Carly continued to appear lost. "I'm Quinton's sister."

"You're not my aunt," Carly said.

Shelby smiled. "I will be."

A gnawing began at the pit of Beth's stomach. She'd never considered this possibility when she'd told Babs that she and Quinton were engaged. She'd jumped in without thinking. When would she learn?

"Mommy?" Carly turned toward Beth as though seeking guidance, and panic filled Beth.

"You're going to be in two weddings," Babs told Carly. "Your aunt Shelby's and then your mommy's."

Dear Lord. "We haven't told her," Beth said.

Indignant, Babs shook her head. "Why on earth not? You're making me an instant grandmother. At the very least, your daughter should know that her mother is getting married."

"You're getting married?" Carly clapped her hands anew. "My mommy's getting married!" she said to Jena.

Beth felt as confused as Jena looked. Just how would she get out of this one?

Carly suddenly turned back to Beth. "Mommy?"

"Yes, honey."

A small wrinkle formed between Carly's blond eyebrows. "Mommy, who are you marrying?"

THREE HOURS LATER, Beth and Quinton were finally alone and able to talk. Beth winced as she shifted under the quilt. She'd probably overdone it, and the stress of her marriage announcement hadn't helped with her recovery.

Carly hadn't wanted to do anything but hug Quinton and practice being a flower girl. She'd done both endlessly the rest of the evening until Beth's nerves had stretched thin. Oh, to be four years old, when the world was simple. But it wasn't simple. Not anymore. Not to Beth. Her farce of an engagement had ensured that.

Beth needed twenty minutes extra to finally get Carly into bed. Then she retired herself.

"Hey." Quinton knocked on Beth's bedroom door. He pushed it open a little. "I brought you a cup of tea."

"Come in," Beth said.

He entered the room, walked to her bedside and sat down next to her, causing the bed to dip under his weight. He handed her the mug. The ceramic warmed her hands.

"Thanks," she said.

His eyes narrowed as he appraised her. "How are you feeling? You appear peaked."

"I'm wondering what we just got ourselves into," Beth said. She took a sip and the tea soothed her throat. "I certainly wasn't expecting this."

"Me, neither." He smiled tenderly. "When you walked across the room, kissed me and told my mother we were engaged, it floored me."

Beth inhaled deeply, then slowly exhaled. The truth was probably best here. At least between them there shouldn't be any lies. "I'm not sure why I did it. I think I wanted to save you the way you saved me. My protective instinct kicked in, maybe."

"Thank you," Quinton said. He took her free hand in his, he raised it to his lips and kissed the back of it. "I appreciate your rescue."

"I just made the situation worse," Beth said. She withdrew her hand before any more heat fused it to Quinton's. "I didn't want Carly to be dragged into this. I guess I didn't think at all."

"My mother is tenacious when she gets an idea," Quinton said. "I didn't expect her to be so gung-ho, either."

"Carly will love being a flower girl," Beth said. She

sipped her tea. "I don't mind that, I suppose. But I didn't want her to know about us. Well, there is no 'us.' But she thinks there is."

Quinton nodded, his dark hair falling into his face. He pushed it back. "I owe you an apology. This was a dumb idea. I never should have planted it in your mind in the first place. The fault is all mine."

"It's mine, too. I said no. I shouldn't have changed my mind tonight."

"It doesn't matter whose fault it is." Quinton took the teacup from her hand and set it on the bedside table. "We've created a situation here that we need to deal with. Shall we come clean?"

Wasn't it too late? "Can we?"

"We can do anything," Quinton said. He nodded. "Seriously. It's up to us."

Beth sighed as sudden guilt consumed her. What would she tell Carly?

"What's wrong?" Quinton asked.

"Did you see Carly's face? She wants to be a flower girl. She hasn't ever gotten to do anything like that before."

"So let her do it. We'll just say we've decided to wait on our wedding until next winter. That'll give us plenty of time to come clean later."

"I can't stay here, though," Beth said. "As soon as I can get back to work, I have to move out."

Quinton's smile cajoled. "It's all going to be okay, Beth. You don't have to move out. You're finally getting better, and by staying here you'll save money. I have plenty of room, and this way you're back on your feet a lot sooner."

"But it means that I'm dependent on you," Beth said. "I don't like that. I'd rather be on my own, even though being financially stable may take longer."

"We're making a trade. You're helping me out with my family."

Didn't he understand? "You make it sound so simple, but it's not. My daughter adores you. How's it going to be when we leave? She thinks we're getting married. What happens when she calls you Dad?"

Quinton held up his hands to calm her. "Beth, we won't let it get that far. And we're becoming friends. When you move out, we'll still be friends. I don't plan on not seeing you ever again. I would like to see you again."

His words spread warmth through her and Beth shook her head vigorously to dissipate it. "I wish I could believe that, but I can't. I've already relied on you too much."

"And you can some more. You've depended on yourself for too long. You have me for as long as you need me."

Quinton handed Beth the mug again and she took a long sip.

She wished she did in fact have Quinton Searle. But Beth was a realist. Despite his assurances, she knew she didn't *have* him—not for long, anyway. And when she did move out, which would be in the very near future, she would go back to her own world. A world in which he didn't exist, couldn't exist. Their worlds were too different.

Quinton's world was wealth and privilege, something Babs Searle had made perfectly clear without saying any words. Beth's world was eking out an existence. Fairy tales were for Carly, not for her. She was too grown-up, too jaded.

Quinton's fingers touched hers as he lifted the ceramic mug from her hand. "Get some rest. We'll deal with my family next weekend. Tell you what. Let's go out to dinner tomorrow. Just the two of us. You probably have cabin fever and should leave the apartment for some fresh scenery. Besides, it'll give us a chance to talk."

"I don't think that's a good idea," Beth said.

"I do." Quinton covered her hands with his. "Tomorrow is Saturday night. Let's have dinner, maybe do a movie. I already asked Jena, and she said she'd baby-sit."

Beth opened her mouth to protest, but Quinton put a finger against her lips to silence her. Her lips quivered under his tender touch and it was all she could do to stop emotions from consuming her.

"Shh. Mull it over," Quinton said, his tone soft, enticing. "You can try all your excuses on me tomorrow."

Mute, she could only nod.

"Great. Then that's settled."

He rose to his feet, the edge of the bed returning to its normal height as his six-foot-three bulk lifted. The room seemed to chill as he moved away from her.

"I'm on duty at work tomorrow. It's also my day to

do hospital rounds. So I won't be home until about four. See you then. We'll have an early night, I'll make reservations for six or six-thirty."

"Okay," Beth said.

Quinton retrieved the mug and gave her a parting smile before he closed the door to her bedroom behind him.

Beth fisted the covers as soon as she heard his footsteps travel down the hall. Tonight, when Beth had tucked Carly in, the little girl had told her, "He's your prince."

A small tear formed and Beth angrily brushed it away. Princes weren't real. As soon as Shelby's wedding was over she was moving out. She couldn't stay any longer. She'd make some phone calls tomorrow. She had a daughter to protect.

Worse, she had herself to protect.

If she didn't, she might begin to believe that the fairy tale that was Dr. Quinton Searle IV might somehow become real.

BETH GAVE HER LIPS one last swipe with her lipstick before recessing the color into the silver tube. Then she reached for a piece of toilet paper, puckered and blotted the excess. She shook her head at the image reflected back at her by the mirror. The pretty rosy shade on her lips gave her an exaggerated pout, the subdued smoky gray eyeliner made her eyes seem wider, and thick black lashes curled and made her eyes look larger.

No wonder she didn't wear makeup much. One, it sweated off in the heat of Luie's kitchen. Two, it made her appear more glamorous than the reality of her life. She blinked, double-checking that the pretty woman staring back so doubtfully was really her.

Although, when she stopped to think about it, why was she making a fuss? Why did she have this sudden feeling of insecurity? Dinner with Quinton shouldn't give her these butterflies in her stomach. After all, he'd seen her stripping for men, fainting, lounging about his apartment in nothing but old, baggy sweats sans makeup.

Just because they were going to a fancy restaurant and she'd put on the absolute best dress she owned, that didn't mean anything. They were simply negotiating a deal, getting to know each other to make a charade work.

She sighed. She wasn't worried about embarrassing him or herself; so, that wasn't the cause of her nervousness. Although she wasn't from Quinton's community circle, Beth had been raised with manners and social graces. She knew how to eat out, what fork to use and all that. So she had no reason to be edgy. This wasn't a date, it was only one event in a surreal world where she existed temporarily. Come two weeks from now, when the job of being Quinton's fiancée was finished, she and Carly would move out and her life would get back to normal. While it might not have the amenities of Quinton's wealth, her life would once again be her own.

She'd talked to her boss, Nancy, earlier and told her that she planned on working Monday. Then next week she would look for a new apartment and perhaps even sign up for spring classes at the college if she could get financial aid. By summer she hoped to be totally back on her feet. That was her resolution.

It was not to fall for Quinton Searle.

"You look pretty, Mommy." Carly bounced into the bathroom. She reached for the tube of lipstick Beth had placed on the counter. "Me, too." Carly made kissing noises. "Me, too."

Beth held out her hand. "Okay, but just for tonight. And who puts lipstick on?"

Her expression turning serious, Carly placed the tube in Beth's palm. "Mommies. I'm never to open the tube myself. I could break it."

"Exactly." Beth took off the tube top, spiraled the lipstick up, then dabbed some on Carly's puckered lips. She set down the tube and Carly smacked her lips. Then Carly executed a few poses in front of the mirror.

"I'm pretty," she said.

"Of course you are," Beth agreed. She ruffled her daughter's hair. "You got all your good looks from me."

Carly's smile widened so that it covered her whole face. "I bet Quinton will think you're pretty. You are very pretty, Mommy."

Hearing her daughter's words, Beth glanced again at her reflection. Who was she trying to kid? She'd worn the dress and applied makeup not because she had to. As she'd pointed out to herself earlier, Quinton had seen her much worse. But she'd still gussied herself up. Deep down she wanted Quinton to find her pretty, to see her as an attractive female. She had to admit the truth to herself—that was what she hoped for.

Years had gone by since she'd been to a nice restaurant. She and Randy hadn't be able to afford such things, not once Carly was on the way. And after he'd gotten sick, even eating from the McDonald's menu was considered luxury.

So tonight she wanted to look her best. And she wanted a man of Quinton Searle's caliber to think she was pretty and attractive in the "I want you, and I'd let you meet my mother" way. She wanted to feel attractive to a handsome man.

Perhaps that made her egotistical or self-centered. She wasn't sure of the exact word. But she'd been with Randy for two years when she'd become pregnant with Carly, and then married. Any man aside from Randy being interested in her—well, that was simply a foreign concept. No one ever had been. She certainly didn't count the men who hooted at her during her rare stripping gigs.

So what if she wanted Quinton to notice her? Quinton was safe. She knew exactly where things stood between them. A little ego massage couldn't hurt. Right?

A tap on the bathroom door sounded, followed by Quinton's voice. "How are we doing?" he asked.

Carly tossed open the door and Beth darted behind it.

"Mommy's pretty," Carly solemnly announced.

"Of course your mom's pretty," Quinton responded.

From behind the door Beth gave him brownie points for being politically correct. She moved her head so she could see around the door without being noticed herself.

"Un-uh. My mommy's really pretty," Carly said. "She put on makeup. See mine?"

"You have lipstick on," Quinton said. "Why, look at those pretty lips. I do believe you might be prettier than your mommy."

Carly preened and struck a few more poses. "I am a princess!" Carly said.

"Of course you are," Quinton said. "So where is your mommy, o, pretty princess?"

"She'd hiding behind the door," Carly answered.

Beth pulled her head back and inwardly groaned.

"I'm not quite ready yet," she called. "How about you two vamoose and leave me alone for a few more minutes."

"That's our cue to leave," Quinton told Carly. "Come on. We'll let her finish becoming beautiful."

"But she's already beautiful," Carly said, her proud words touching Beth's heart.

"Of course she is," Quinton said. "But she needs privacy."

"Okay."

Beth saw Carly's feet disappear from view. Then Beth stepped out and closed the bathroom door. She glanced at herself in the mirror. Although the dress wasn't the latest fashion, the simplicity of the lines made the garment timeless. The gray flannel fabric hugged her curves, and the dress dropped to her ankles. The scooped neck of the bodice covered yet emphasized cleavage, and the long sleeves were tight and fitted to Beth's wrist. She had accessorized the dress with a simple black-, red-, white-and-gray scarf. Nervousness again claimed her. Maybe just a dab more mascara and a smidgen more blush. That should do it.

"We need to leave in ten minutes," Quinton called back.

Her reflection mirrored her innermost fears. Was this how Cinderella felt? All tingly and ready to take a walk outside her measly world? Carly had declared Quinton as handsome as Prince Eric in Disney's *The Little Mermaid*. But Quinton was no prince…

"Did you hear me?" Quinton asked, his voice suddenly close.

He was just on the other side of the door, and Beth could feel his presence.

She stepped backward even though he couldn't see her. "Don't worry. I'll be ready."

She heard him sigh with relief. "Great. Sorry if I'm sounding like a nag. My sister and mother always take forever, and without reminders they'd make everyone late. I just want to be sure we get our table. Oh, there's the doorbell. Jena's here. I'll see you in a few."

Beth heard the sound of his footsteps fade as he moved away. Her hand shook slightly as she reached for the compact. Methodically she sponged a tad more blush on her cheeks. No, she wasn't a princess. And she had to be her own fairy godmother. But for tonight she would let herself go to the party and have fun. She'd forget the real world she existed in. Just for tonight…

If only for tonight.

Just one little taste wouldn't spoil her forever.

She wouldn't let it.

Chapter Five

Quinton followed Carly into the living room. Jena had just arrived, and Carly bounded over.

"Look, Jena, I'm pretty. I'm wearing lipstick."

"Ooh," Jena said.

Quinton glanced at his watch. Why was he so nervous? Jena had baby-sat before, and he and Beth had been alone. Heck, she'd fainted into his arms.

But they hadn't been on a date.

If that was even what this was. No. It wasn't a date. It was simply two people going out to a nice restaurant for good food, good conversation and a chance to get to know each other in a new setting.

And they had an ulterior motive, too, so that definitely made it not a date.

Although his mother realized that Beth and Quinton had just met, and that much was true, she'd expect them to really be familiar with each other. Despite the amount of time Beth had lived in his apartment, Quinton didn't necessarily understand her well. He knew she'd been married, and that her husband died. He knew the medical bills Beth had endured paying because of her husband's death had been huge. He knew she made cakes and pies and occasionally delivered food for Luie's Deli. She was Carly's mother, and she loved her daughter. But he really didn't know *her*, who she was inside and how she thought.

Quinton still didn't like the fact that Beth had needed money so badly she'd been ready to strip for it, but after seeing her devotion to Carly and how much Beth cared, Quinton could understand the desperation and determination to provide for her daughter that had been the prime motivation behind the stripping.

As for her living with him, again her motivation had been to provide for her daughter.

So it wasn't a date. They were just two people wanting something from each other—sort of like Edward and Vivian in the movie *Pretty Woman.* As long as he didn't do something dumb like kiss her again or fall for Beth, life would be fine.

"I'm ready."

At the sound of Beth's voice, Quinton turned. It had only been a movie, but Quinton now knew how Edward felt when he saw Vivian that first time in the bar after Vivian had been all cleaned up.

The character Julia Roberts had portrayed had been beautiful, but she didn't compare with Beth. She wore low pumps, and as she stepped forward, her ankle wobbled.

Instantly Quinton reached her side. He cupped her elbow, her body through the gray flannel fabric warm to his touch. Amazingly, he still had a voice. "Shall we go?" he asked.

"Yes," Beth said.

Quinton stepped aside and his fingers missed touching her. He watched as Carly gave her mother one last kiss. Carly's arms snaked up as high as she could reach and she pressed her head into her mother's legs.

"Bye, Mom."

"Kisses," Beth said.

Carly turned her face up and Beth leaned down. The touch of her lips to her daughter's was light and brief, but it still managed to tug at something deep inside Quinton.

"You be a good girl for Jena," Beth said.

"I will," Carly said dutifully.

"Good night," Beth said, and she moved next to Quinton.

Jena and Carly clapped as they left.

"She's cute," Quinton said when they were out of earshot.

"I like to think so," Beth said.

Rare nervousness overtook Quinton as they stepped into the elevator. How long had it been since he'd had a date? Not that long ago—and he certainly hadn't been this nervous. The elevator made a stop, and with another couple in the elevator the ensuing silence felt more normal.

Once in the parking garage, Quinton opened Beth's door and seated her inside the Mercedes sedan. "We're going to Fanetta," he told Beth. "It's French."

"Sounds wonderful," Beth said. As they drove, she turned to stare out the tinted passenger window at Lake Shore Drive. Quinton headed north, and about ten minutes later he turned into another parking garage.

"We're here." He helped her from the car, led her to an elevator, and then hit the button for the top floor.

When Beth stepped out, she gasped. The restaurant was beautiful. She'd seen scenes like it in the daytime soaps, but never before had she been in such a place. The hostess greeted them and led them through a vine-covered arbor. Discreetly placed tables ringed an intimate dance floor where a miniaturized version of a big band played. Some people danced; others held hushed conversations. The hostess led them past several tables into an out-of-the-way corner. The view out both windows was "nothing but" Lake Michigan to the east and the downtown Chicago skyline to the south.

Quinton saw her fascination as he pushed the chair in. "This okay?"

"It's wonderful," Beth said. She'd never been anywhere like it. She didn't even have to look at the menu to know that every item had to be pricey. The ambience alone said so.

Quinton seated himself just to her right so that both of them had a panoramic view. Beth could see the lights of the Drake Hotel.

"Wine?" Quinton asked. He'd picked up the wine menu.

"I don't know if I should. Having been sick and all," she said.

"A glass won't hurt if you want one," Quinton said. "But as a doctor, I wouldn't advise more."

"A glass, then," Beth agreed. Wine had been a luxury she'd forgone for what seemed like forever. A glass sounded divine.

He tilted his head and looked at her. "Do you have a preference?"

She paused. She loved a variety of reds and semi-dry whites. But if she was going to indulge... "A merlot," she said.

"Done," Quinton told her.

As the wine steward came to their table, Beth watched as Quinton held a serious and educated discussion with the man before choosing a vintage.

When her glass arrived, Beth had to admit the wine was the smoothest she'd ever tasted. Time lost meaning, and before Beth even cracked open her menu, a waiter appeared and Quinton chose baked Brie and escargots as appetizers. He shot her a look when the waiter disappeared to place the order.

"What, never had snails before?"

She shook her head, her blond hair swishing about her shoulders. "I can't say that's on the menu at Luie's."

His gray eyes twinkled and Beth flushed under his appraisal.

"Then they'll be a new experience for you. I like them much better than caviar. Probably because they'll be drenched in butter."

To calm herself, Beth took a sip of her delicious wine. "And you're supposed to be a doctor."

"My cholesterol is fine. I don't get to eat escargots much. They'll go well with the wine, and I did order us some Perrier water, as well."

She also had never had that beverage. "Okay," she said. To alleviate her nervousness, she smoothed out a wrinkle in the linen napkin the waiter had placed in her lap. That was safer than guzzling her wine.

"So, do you trust me?" His tone was light, but his eyes held a challenge.

"I think so," Beth said honestly. And why not? She knew why he'd brought her here, that everything was part of his master plan for them to fool his parents. And he wasn't trying to seduce her or woo her. So far Quinton, unlike Randy, had been a man of his word.

"You *can* trust me," Quinton reaffirmed.

His gray eyes seemed unfathomable, and then he smiled, the wide grin breaking the tension between them. Her relief lasted all of a second, until he said, "So tell me about Beth Johnson."

"There's not really much to tell."

He arched an eyebrow. "Surely there's something."

She hated to break the night's fantasy with the reality of her meager life. "No."

He didn't buy it. "Nothing?"

Refusing to part with being Cinderella until at least the stroke of midnight, she shook her head, once again sending her hair swishing. "*Nada.* Tell you what. You start and that'll give me time to make up something much more interesting."

Quinton chuckled. "Okay, although you have nothing to fear. My life is boring. Eldest child. Went to private high school. Went to Northwestern for both undergraduate and medical school. I completed residency, all my requirements for my license, got the job I have now, became board certified, and that's about it. A very short story."

"No lady loves?" She put a hand to her lips. "Sorry. I shouldn't have asked that."

Quinton shook his head. "It's fine. My mother would expect you to be privy to all that. And the answer is no. None serious. I've been too busy, I suppose."

His face clouded for a moment. "Medical school and internship are hard, nonstop work. And I suppose no one held my interest enough to make my priorities change, to make me less self-absorbed in becoming a doctor worthy of filling my father's shoes."

"Hence your mother's being desperate to marry you off."

"That and taking over my father's practice. He really should simply turn it over to his partners, but he's stubborn. I'm out of St. Louis, and I want to stay out."

The finality in his tone made Beth curious. "What's so wrong with St. Louis?"

Quinton frowned. "I..." He paused, and as if on cue the waiter approached.

"Have you decided?" he asked.

Beth picked up the menu. She hadn't even opened it. Perhaps she hadn't wanted to know how much things cost, how much Quinton was paying. She could never afford a place like this; perhaps part of the fantasy should be in the unknown. "Why don't you order for me," she suggested. "I'm game for anything."

Quinton assessed her for a second and then nodded. "I can do that." He raised his gaze to the waiter. "We'll have the chateaubriand for two. Medium. House dressing on the salad and house potatoes."

"An excellent choice," the waiter said. He disappeared again.

"It sounds wonderful," Beth admitted.

"You'll like it," Quinton said. "I split it with my sister last time, in case you're wondering."

Beth colored slightly. She *had* been wondering, but she hadn't wanted to ask.

"It's a twenty-ounce center-cut tenderloin that will come with béarnaise sauce, duchess potatoes and some steamed vegetables. I hope medium is fine," he said.

"Yes," Beth said. The basket of French bread that had appeared with the escargots had magically refilled itself. She reached for a slice and set the warm piece on her bread plate. "You avoided my question, you realize. Why don't you want to return to St. Louis?"

Quinton froze, his butter knife in midair. He set it down on his plate. "I'm Fred Searle's son."

"I don't get it."

"My father is Quinton Frederick the third. He goes by Fred. I got stuck with Quinton."

"Oh. Okay. But that doesn't explain why..."

He frowned. "No, it probably doesn't. In a nutshell, St. Louis is a small town when it comes to who's who in society. My parents are on that mythical A-list. I learned in high school that it was meaningless."

He paused, and Beth instantly understood that the memory was hard for him. He sipped his wine before continuing.

"I liked this girl, and everyone had a bet on her. All the guys were trying to pick her up and she went out onto the golf course with me. Nothing happened. We talked. I kissed her once. I promised to call. I actually liked her. She might have been rich, but was too brainy, too plain for the guys at my school. When we came back in, the guys asked me what happened, and while I didn't lie, I didn't tell the truth. I thought I was protecting her and she never would be the wiser since school was over. She overheard all their congratulations on winning the bet."

"Oh, my," Beth said.

"Yeah," Quinton said. "Not one of my better moments and I've since apologized. She's happily married now. But that's not the point. The point is that I'm Fred's son. I go back, take over the practice, and I'll have a certain role to fill, a certain image to maintain. I have no desire to fill that role. I've freed myself from those people and their narrow-mindedness. I don't want it. I'm not in that world anymore."

"Which is where I come in."

"Yeah, I guess so. My pretend fiancée who will keep my family at bay."

The escargots were delicious, and Beth finished a bite before replying. "I'll try. But I don't think your mother approved of me."

"Not to sound rude, but she didn't." He looked sheepish. "Not that that will stop her. She wants me wed."

Beth laughed, although when she thought about it, deep down it wasn't funny. Ironic, maybe, and when one really thought about it, cruel. Quinton's mother had judged her and found her lacking on the acceptability scale. "Well, I guess you didn't *want* someone your mother would have liked," Beth said.

Quinton used his left hand to cover her right one. His touch at once soothed and spelled danger. Beth tried to pull her hand away.

"Don't."

His tone was sharp and she stilled her hand.

"I can just imagine what's in your mind right now, and you are wrong. You are a wonderful woman, Beth, and I mean that. I'm enjoying getting to know you, exploring our being friends. Don't let my mother affect you. Don't let her bring you down. That's why I'm in Chicago—to escape from all those preconceived notions. I'm not like that. I'm not a snob. I don't see class differences. I only see a lovely woman seated across from me, one who is very strong and brave."

How Beth wanted to believe that. But she knew better. Even though he was a man of his word, he'd seen the real her. He'd seen her stripping, desperate for money. She made pies for a living. She had a failed marriage under her belt. She was Beth Johnson, girl without a degree or a high-paying job. She'd almost landed in the shelter.

Sure, she was strong. Sure, she was a survivor.

And surviving meant not believing in fantasies, in not opening herself up for pain and heartbreak.

Their salads arrived, ending all serious conversation. For the rest of dinner, she and Quinton talked on broad topics such as politics and philosophy. The delicious main course followed the salads, and Beth memorized the flavor and texture of every morsel. She reveled in the decadency and delectableness of it all. After all, who knew when she'd ever eat like this again.

"So?" Quinton placed the linen napkin on the table. A waiter whisked it and his empty plate away. "Did you enjoy it?"

"Excellent," Beth said. And it had been. Her stomach felt so full; she had eaten every last bit of the delicious food. "I haven't had a meal like this in quite a long time."

"We'll have to do more of them." He saw her sigh. "As friends," he added quickly.

Friends. Impossible in their different worlds. As if she could afford a restaurant like this. "Quinton."

His lip lowered slightly at her gentle yet reproving tone. "Okay, we won't talk about a future."

"Good," Beth said, for even as friends, they had no future. She wasn't from this world, and the sooner she got her daughter away from it, the better off everyone would be. Tonight was all the fantasy she would allow herself.

"You will dance with me, though, won't you?"

"They're ballroom-dancing," she said. "Waltzing."

Quinton rose to his feet. "I had lessons. Let me tell you what a joy that was. That said, we're not dancing like that. We're going to Weeble."

She tilted her head and stared at him. "Weeble?"

He grinned and reached for her hand. His touch tantalized as she followed him toward the dance floor.

"Weeble. Remember those little round children's toys? 'Weebles wobble, but they don't fall down'? We're going to do the Weeble."

They stepped onto the dance floor and Quinton turned to her. "You just put your arms around me like this—" Quinton guided Beth's hands to his shoulders "—now I put my arms around you like this—" Quinton's hands circled her waist.

Beth trembled as he drew her to him.

"Now we simply step and sway. The Weeble."

"We're slow-dancing," she said.

He grinned. "Exactly. Weebling."

He led easily, and Beth slowly relaxed. How could she not? She was in Quinton's warm, secure embrace. If she leaned forward slightly she could rest her head on his chest. Even from her current position she could hear the rhythmic thumping of his heart. She leaned forward, and her ear touched the soft fabric of his shirt.

As they danced, rare peace settled over her. Raw passion for Randy had gotten her into her predicament. But being in Quinton's arms wasn't about lust, a need to possess someone and have someone belong to you. With Quinton, she felt a partnership. A togetherness. A perfect fit.

She felt as though she belonged right there in his arms, as though those arms had been made to hold her. Yet that couldn't be further from the truth.

Had Cinderella experienced this conflict? Had she cared?

But Beth wasn't Cinderella and never would be. She stiffened. Quinton must have felt her tense.

"Shh," he said against the top of her head. She'd worn her hair loose, and one of his hands left her waist and slid under the strands. He kneaded the back of her neck. "Don't pull away," he whispered. "I'm enjoying this."

She was, too, and that was the problem. *Never get used to what you can't have again,* said a voice inside her. As the band began another number, she drew away. "I'm tired," she said by way of excuse.

"Okay." His concern was evident and he leaned back and studied her face. "You are a little flushed. You haven't been well all that long. Let's sit down. I could use some coffee before we go."

When Beth nodded, Quinton guided her toward the table.

"Quinton?"

Hearing the unfamiliar voice, Beth paused. A gentleman in his early sixties was coming their way, a large smile on his face.

"Quinton, good to see you."

"Hey, Bart." Quinton's left hand still rested on Beth's back and he shook the man's hand with his right. "Beth, this is one of the partners in the pediatric practice I belong to. Bart Zimmerman, this is Beth Johnson."

Beth smiled and shook Bart's hand.

He gazed at her for a moment. "So you're the one," the man said. "You have good taste, Quinton."

The one? Beth's brain echoed as her heart missed a beat. Did he recognize her from the bachelor party? Good grief, she'd started taking off her clothes for Quinton's colleagues. Even if Bart hadn't been there, the gossip had surely gotten around Quinton's office about how he'd accosted the stripper and taken her away. She hadn't considered that anyone would recognize her. She really hadn't been at the party long enough for anyone to fully see her face.

"Yes, you're the one. Quinton's new love." Bart beamed. "You'll have to come meet my wife. It's our fortieth wedding anniversary tomorrow and we're celebrating tonight."

"Really, we don't want to intrude…" Quinton began to politely refuse Bart's invitation.

Bart made a dismissive gesture with his hand. "Oh, you're not intruding. You'll be doing me a favor. You know that anniversary or not, Margaret would kill me, Quinton, if I didn't introduce her to your fiancée. It's a pleasure to meet you, my dear."

Beth sighed with relief. Bart hadn't recognized her. If he had, his social politeness to Quinton's fiancée would preclude mentioning it.

At Bart's words, though, Quinton winced. He felt as though someone had just sucker-punched him.

Everyone at work knew he was engaged? While that, perhaps, was somehow part of the ill-laid plan he and Beth had concocted, he hadn't expected the news of his "engagement" to travel so fast. He stared at Bart.

"How did you find out?"

"From a third party." Bart gave an overdone dramatic sigh, as if he'd been slighted.

Quinton's fingers tensed where they rested on Beth's back. "We just told my family last night."

Bart's smile broadened. "Well, you know what they say about good news traveling fast. And of course I'm just giving you grief by pretending to be offended. I'm delighted for you. Your mother told my wife. So you must come introduce Beth to Margaret."

Quinton kept a polite smile plastered on his face. His mother wasn't just spreading the news; she was probably also digging for information. More than likely she'd called everyone in her Rolodex for details about Quinton's fiancée… But right now the issue was Quinton and Beth being coerced into meeting Bart's wife.

"We'd be delighted to say hello to Margaret," Quinton said finally. He moved his fingers from Beth's back and cupped her elbow. "But we can only stay a moment or two. Beth hasn't been feeling too well lately and this is her first night out in a while. Right, honey?"

Beth still appeared a little shell-shocked, but to her credit, she recovered quickly. "Right," she said.

When Bart turned and led the way, she followed.

Within seconds the awkward introductions were over and Quinton escorted Beth back to their table. His hands grazed her shoulders as he pushed her chair in. The waiter appeared with a silver coffee urn.

"Cream or sugar?" he asked.

"Black," Quinton said. At this moment the bitter balm probably couldn't be dark enough for him. Beth's mood had shifted since the dance. She'd tensed and withdrawn. He didn't like it. He'd wanted a night to explore who she was without the distraction of their "arrangement." Instead, they'd become further embroiled in their deception. He wanted the fun Beth he'd seen earlier in the evening, but she'd slipped away.

"Some for you, miss?"

"No. No, thank you," Beth said.

She leaned on her elbows and stared at Quinton as he sipped his coffee. He glanced over at her, but her face was unreadable. Just what was on her mind? He shifted uncomfortably.

"Am I doing something wrong?" He gave her a quizzical smile as he held up the tiny porcelain cup. "I realize this probably looks ridiculous. I prefer a big mug of coffee, not these little dainty cups."

Her mouth turned upward wearily as she attempted to reassure him. "You're fine. I'm just suddenly really tired, that's all," she said.

"Then we'll go." Quinton put down the cup and made a discreet gesture with his left wrist. The waiter, understanding the request for the bill, nodded.

"Don't rush on my account," Beth said. She pointed to his cup. "Finish your coffee."

Quinton shook his head. "I can make a pot at home.

I don't want you wearing yourself down. You just said you were tired. The last thing you need is to overdo it."

Beth sighed. "I agree. I probably should rest. I'm planning on going back to work Monday."

Quinton's hand stilled on his cup. She was going back to work? The thought didn't sit well at all and he felt a twinge of concern in his stomach. He struggled to keep his face neutral and his voice calm, although calm wasn't what he was feeling. Anxiety was more like it. It hadn't been that long since she'd collapsed in his arms.

"Are you sure you want to go back to work already?"

"Yes," she said.

He assessed her. A rosiness had returned to her skin, but there were worry lines around her eyes that hadn't been visible earlier. He sucked in his breath and then exhaled it in a rush.

"Are you sure you're ready to go back? I have to admit that I don't like it."

Beth straightened and leaned back in the chair. She pushed a wayward strand of hair back from her face. Quinton had the sudden itch to touch that blond hair.

"I don't want to leave Nancy shorthanded. Customers depend on Luie's for their family dinner—you'd be amazed at the loyalty of the clientele. Which means I've got dozens of pastries to bake. I called Nancy earlier today and told her I'd be in. I also called Ida, and she's missed Carly. She said she'd be happy to watch her for a few days."

"So that's it. It's back to work." The statement came out flat. But an unspoken accusation hung in the air. He shouldn't care. He wasn't Beth's nursemaid. They had a plan, an engagement of convenience. As soon as they saw it through, she'd be on with her own life and he on with his.

Simple. Foolproof. Perfect.

He found himself not stomaching that idea one iota.

The waiter appeared at his side, and glad for the diversion, Quinton reached for the brown leather folder the waiter had placed on the corner of the table. No more than five minutes later, he and Beth were in the car and on their way back to the apartment.

"The lakefront is pretty," she said, her voice breaking the odd silence that permeated the car.

Now, here was a comfortable topic. "I love it," Quinton said. His hands on the steering wheel, he negotiated Lake Shore Drive's never-ending traffic. "In the summer I keep my boat over in that marina."

"Really? You have a boat?" Beth craned her neck to her right.

Because it was dark, he knew she really couldn't see anything. "A sailboat," Quinton said. "I'll have to take you and Carly out on it this summer." So much for safe topics. He realized his mistake the minute the words left his lips. Would she even be speaking to him six months from now? She seemed to have everything planned about work and all. He didn't like it. On the dance floor he thought he'd felt something stir. He'd held her in his arms and... But to Beth, he was simply a housemate, an acquaintance, a partner in deception. "I mean, we'll still be friends?"

"Sure," Beth said, a bit too quickly.

How dumb could he get? She didn't want him. What was that cliché? In for a penny, in for a pound? "The lake's really great. It's 321 miles long, 22,400 square miles. With quite a few wrecks out there, too. The *Lady Elgin,* the *J. Loomis McLaren* and the *Wells Burt* are all pretty close together—well, relatively speaking. I don't know why exactly, but they all sank in the mid to late 1800s."

"I have no idea, either," Beth said. "I've never been a tourist in my own town. I think Carly has seen more of Chicago in this past week than I have in my entire life. I've never been in the Sears Tower."

They exited Lake Shore Drive and turned onto Michigan Avenue. "You'll have to change that," Quinton said.

"Easier said than done," Beth said. "Leisure time is not a commodity I have a lot of."

He didn't quite know how to answer that. He'd endured medical school and internship and all the hours that went with them. He had a practice that could consume his time. But he still made time for himself.

Then again, he didn't have a child to consider. He didn't even have a pet. He could take off and leave at a moment's notice. And now he could schedule his hours so that he had plenty of recreational time. One of the partners in the practice loved snow skiing, while Quinton loved to sail. They had an arrangement, Quinton worked more in the winter and less in the summer.

"Hopefully you'll get to take some time to enjoy Chicago," Quinton finished lamely. He put on his turn signal, and as soon as traffic cleared, he drove into the underground parking garage of his building.

"We'll see," Beth said.

The rest of the way to the apartment they endured another, awkward silence. Quinton wasn't quite sure what to do, what to say.

"Did you have a good evening?" Jena asked when they entered the apartment.

"Wonderful," Beth said, then changed the subject. "How was Carly?"

"An angel like always," Jena said. "She's a great little girl."

"Thanks." Beth hung her coat up before Quinton could be chivalrous and take it from her. "I'm going to check on her. Thanks Jena. Good night."

"'Night," Jena said. She turned and looked expectantly at Quinton as soon as Beth had left. "Well? How was it?"

"Fine." Quinton shrugged out of his overcoat.

Jena frowned slightly. "That doesn't sound like two happy lovebirds who had a great time on a first date."

For a date, first or otherwise, the end had been a bust. Quinton sighed. "We're not two lovebirds. We're two roommates who are pretending to be engaged so that my family gets off my case about marriage. Unfortunately my mother called Bart's wife, and now it's all over the office that I'm getting married. I'm sure when I go to the hospital next it'll be all over there, too."

"Ooh." Jena had that expression on her face, the one that women get when they don't like something and aren't sure what to say. "I wondered about the suddenness of your engagement. So tell me, whose dumb idea was this?"

"Mine," Quinton admitted. "I suggested it to Beth. But she said no." He paused. "That is, until my family showed up. But you were there as a witness."

"I was. And of course Beth isn't anything that your family would want for you, right?"

Definitely a given. "I don't think my mother was too impressed. But Babs never is too pleased with stuff she's not in control over."

"What about you?"

Quinton frowned. "What about me?"

"You and Beth. You forget I've worked with you for a year now. I've watched you with her. You seem to like her."

He did like her. That wasn't the problem. He brushed off the sense that their relationship might be more. She'd made it clear tonight that it wouldn't be.

"I do. As a friend. That's all. She's not my type, Jena."

The words sounded hollow even to his ears. Not surprisingly, Jena jumped all over him.

"Do you even know what your type is?" she asked.

His guy defense system kicking into high gear, he bristled. "I'll know it when I see it, and Beth isn't it. I know it just like I know you aren't it for me and you know I'm not it for you. Beth and I are just helping each other out of a tight spot, that's all."

Jena bit her lip, as if stifling a sharp reply. She shook her head and grabbed her coat. "Either of you hurts that little girl and both of you will have me to deal with."

"No one wants to see anyone hurt," Quinton said. "Especially Carly."

"Good," Jena said, but she didn't seem convinced. If anything, she looked downright skeptical. "I'll see you when you make your rounds next."

Quinton nodded. He'd already given Jena a hefty check for all her baby-sitting services. "Thanks again for baby-sitting."

"I meant what I said," Jena warned. "Take care." With that she was gone.

Quinton strode over to the northern windows, stepping over one of Carly's dolls as he did so. He pressed his hands to the window feeling the winter chill that tried to seep through the insulated panes. Out there, beneath the city lights, was the cold, choppy lake. He wished his boat weren't in dry dock, that it was summer, that he could row out to it, hoist the sail and disappear into the blue. He needed escape.

His cell phone shrilled, and he reached into his pocket for it. Who would be calling at nine o'clock at night? The beast had been mercifully silent all evening and he wasn't on call tonight. Quinton groaned as he saw the number. He pressed the send button and accepted the call.

"I was just thinking about a June wedding for you and Beth," a familiar voice said.

What a mess this situation was becoming. "Hello, Mom," he said.

Chapter Six

"So how's living with that sexy doctor working out? Any sparks flying? Does he want to do any examinations of your body? You know, the up-close-and-personal kind?"

"Nancy." Beth's voice conveyed firm warning, but her boss of the past year ignored it.

"I mean, even though you'd called me and told me that today was the day you were coming back to work, I didn't believe it until I saw you walk in those doors. If I were shacked up with that sexy hunk of yours I wouldn't want to—"

"He's not my hunk," Beth interrupted as she reached for the flour and began to measure out another cupful. She didn't make her pie crust in bulk, but instead ran several commercial mixers simultaneously. Each mixer contained enough dough for one pie crust. Today Beth would fill the crusts with a German-chocolate batter.

Her boss waited until Beth had started each mixer before saying, "What do you mean, he's not your hunk? He came in here, said you were ill and that you were living with him. I'd never seen a man so concerned. And those gray eyes of his. Amazing. Don't you just love them? I would drown in them."

Beth didn't want to think about Quinton's eyes. Ever since Saturday night those gray orbs had been haunting her dreams. "Nancy, I'm not living with him because he likes me. He just feels guilty. He caused me to lose some money and I couldn't get into my new apartment. So he's allowed me to stay there for a bit. That's all there is to the story. Purely platonic. Just a friend helping out a friend."

Nancy dropped sugar-cookie dough onto parchment-paper-covered baking sheets. She waved the silver scoop. "We've worked together for over a year, Beth. There's more to it than that. You didn't even mention him to me."

"I have lot of friends I don't mention," Beth said. Even though she and Nancy were close colleagues, Beth didn't think that her boss needed to know the real reason Quinton wanted her around. The fact that everyone in his office now thought he was getting married was bad enough. She wanted to bury her crime, not confess it. The whole mess had spiraled out of control.

And control was something Beth wanted at this moment in her life. She needed to be empowered. She needed to be on her own two feet again, no longer living in fear of losing her home. She wanted to be independent, be her own woman, relying on no one but herself.

Yes, the sooner Beth earned some money, the better. She shut off each commercial mixer, turned out the first ball of dough onto the floured steel table and started to roll it flat. She had to concentrate on growing her career, not on Quinton Searle or her misguided desire for him to massage her ego.

That was foolish. Saturday night she'd wanted him to find her attractive. Oh, she'd felt like Cinderella at the ball. She'd danced with a prince. But after the night had ended, he hadn't sought her out. He hadn't wanted her.

He'd even told Jena that Beth wasn't his type. Oh, she'd overheard his words, all right, while on her way to the kitchen.

She'd known what he said was the truth. She had no one to blame but herself for this mess she was in. She had to stop wanting others to give her affirmation. She needed to self-affirm. Still, actually hearing the words had cut deep, bringing up a past of rejection.

She hadn't been Randy's type, either. They'd just been two people trapped in a bad situation. First, they'd stayed in a relationship built on the idea that no one should be alone, years after the magic and chemistry had fizzled and died. Then, she'd been too settled to risk upsetting her life and leaving. She'd been too afraid to start over. And then, she'd gotten pregnant. Carly's birth had brought joy, but financial hardship had tempered that joy as Beth and Randy juggled the costs of Beth's delivery and all Carly's childhood exams. As well, Randy had always blamed Beth for getting pregnant. He'd done the right thing and married her, but even though they'd forged a truce, he'd re-sented her. When Randy got sick, Beth had been further trapped. One should never stay in a bad situation, but Randy was dying and she couldn't leave him then. And now she was free, but the road wasn't easy.

"Those look good," Nancy said as Beth finished rolling the last crust.

"Thanks," Beth said.

"So have you enrolled in your classes yet? I checked the schedule. The quarter starts in March. I'll be able to work around it."

"That's great," Beth said. She placed the crusts in the pans, then fluted the edges perfectly. "I should get up there, or it'll be summer before I know it. I think I'm eligible for some financial aid. I'll need it, especially once I move out of Quinton's."

Nancy gave her a sharp glance. "Beth, I realize this isn't your dream job, but you've established a solid reputation as a pastry chef. I'll be sorry to see you go once you graduate. However, I want what's best for you. Which may just be that guy you claim not to have anything going with. Perhaps you should explore your feelings for him. He seems pretty nice to me, and who knows what six hours in a car to St. Louis can do. I've got you covered for the first two Fridays in February. A little anniversary magic one weekend, and some wedding magic the next weekend, and some romance could happen."

Beth had already prepared the pie filling, and she now poured it into the fluted crusts. "Nothing will happen and I don't want to hear any more about it, Nancy, or I'll leave you with all these pies. He didn't want me to come back to work at all, you know."

"Okay, okay." Nancy grinned. "I won't mention him again. But you'd be a fool not to try for him. After all, you've already got squatter's rights. The man could be perfect father material."

"Nancy!" Beth almost poured in too much batter.

As Nancy removed a sheet of cookies from one of the commercial ovens, she laughed.

BETH FORGOT about the conversation with Nancy until a little over a week later. It was Thursday evening, and she and Quinton were sitting in the McDonald's Play-Place in Normal, the red trays containing their dinners on the blue table in front of them. They were on their way to St. Louis for his parents' anniversary.

"So I guess this is what it's like," Quinton said. He dipped a french fry in ketchup before gesturing with it for emphasis. "This is life in playland."

"Just be glad McDonald's has salads now," Beth said. She forked a piece of grilled-chicken Caesar salad into her mouth. Two children shrieked and ran by before again climbing into the multicolored maze of tubes and tunnels.

Carly squirmed in her chair. "Play," she insisted. "Eat the rest later."

"Okay," Beth said. Carly was off her chair in a flash, her shoes deposited in the cubby as if they had wings and had flown there.

Quinton gestured toward Carly's half-eaten meal. "She's done?"

"No," Beth answered with a shake of her head. "She'll come back a few times and pick at it until it's all gone. PlayPlace ways."

"I see," Quinton said. More children shouted, and the sound echoed in the huge glass enclosure. "It's loud in here."

"Always," Beth acknowledged. "You'll get used to it."

Quinton looked around him and Beth knew what he saw. The place was packed with loud, laughing children all having the time of their lives. Beth guessed that most of the crowd were travelers like Quinton and her.

They'd opted to leave Chicago at night. The hope was that Carly would be asleep for most of the journey. They'd stopped at a McDonald's restaurant for a late dinner and to let Carly stretch her legs and play.

Quinton gazed longingly at the interior of the restaurant, where the glass divider kept the rest of the restaurant mercifully quiet.

"So you think we'll get in about one a.m.?" Beth asked.

"Yes," Quinton said. He checked at his watch. "This shouldn't cost us too much time."

"I can get her…"

Quinton shook his head. "Let her run. I'm contemplating getting an ice-cream sundae."

Beth remembered the steak and escargots from Saturday night and once again commented on his diet. "I thought doctors were supposed to eat healthy."

He arched an eyebrow at her. "What's wrong with ice cream?"

She felt silly, but she'd already dug herself the hole. "You had a quarter pounder with cheese, too."

He grinned. "Ah, she cares for me. I work out daily. I can spare a few fat cells. I don't come here often. It's a great treat to eat fast food. The cafeteria at the hospital serves mostly full home-cooked meals. And at the office it's always subs or salads. The front-desk girls and nurses are always trying to lose weight. So this was a great change."

He nodded toward the tray in front of her. "All you had was a salad. Want a sundae with nuts and whipped cream?" His eyes held a challenge and the gray darkened as his gaze roved over her. "You can spare it, trust me."

Beth flushed under his appraisal. Stress worked the opposite way on her. Instead of feeding her anxiety with food, she often stopped eating altogether. The result was, well, she'd fainted into Quinton's arms the last time. "I'll pass," she said.

Carly ran up at that moment. "I've made a bunch of new friends," she announced. She shoved a few french fries into her mouth, their being cold not bothering her in the slightest. She noticed Quinton was standing. "Where ya goin'?"

"Where are you going?" Beth corrected.

"I'm going to get some ice cream," Quinton said.

Carly's hand stilled above a chicken nugget. "I want some."

"May I have some, please?" Beth said.

"May I have some, please?" Carly repeated.

"Finish your food first," Beth said.

Carly shoved the remnants of the chicken nugget in her mouth. "Now?" she asked, food clearly visible.

Beth closed her mouth. No use in reminding Carly not to talk with her mouth full; at this point the damage was already done.

"Okay," Quinton said. Carly headed to the shoe cubby, grabbed her shoes and quickly secured the Velcro tabs. She skipped back and put her hand in Quinton's.

Beth watched as Quinton's hand seemed to swallow up Carly's little one. Her blond ponytail bobbed as she looked up at Quinton, her face filled with adoration. Hand in hand, they went into the main part of the restaurant.

Beth shifted so that she could see them through the glass. Quinton had lifted Carly up so that she could see the choices. He pointed, she pointed, and then Carly did nod once before she threw her arms around Quinton's neck and gave him a big hug.

A lump formed in Beth's throat and she turned away.

"He looks like a good dad," a voice said.

Beth moved slightly, for the first time noticing a grandmother type who had also observed the whole scene. Beth didn't have the heart to explain. "He is," she said.

Quinton was a natural with kids. And Carly adored him. She'd be devastated when they moved out.

Many people had come and gone in Carly's short life. The most profound, the one with the deepest impact, was her father. Beth didn't have any background in psychology, but her gut told her that little girls, especially those Carly's age, needed male role models. It had something to do with imprinting—the more positive the male influence in a young girl's life, the more positive the relationships she would have with men down the road.

Maybe Beth had heard about it on one of those talk shows. Something about Freudian Oedipal feelings. All Beth knew was that Randy's death had been like one desertion, and leaving Quinton would seem like another.

Quinton and Carly came back with three ice-cream cones. "We got you one, too," Carly said.

"Thank you," Beth said. She took the cone Quinton offered.

"I figured your no meant yes," Quinton told her with a cheeky grin.

Beth licked the soft-serve, the vanilla flavor a welcome finishing touch after the delicious tartness of the Caesar salad dressing. "Okay, you guessed right," she admitted. "But don't think that this means you know me or anything."

His eyes darkened, as if she'd thrown out some unspoken challenge. "Oh, I won't. Believe me, my mama didn't raise a fool."

"You're not a fool," Carly exclaimed. She had ice cream smeared from the tip of her nose to her chin. "Why would you be a fool? Do mommies raise fools? Mommy, am I going to be a fool when I grow up?"

"No, mommies don't raise fools," Quinton answered. He finished his ice-cream cone. "It's just an expression. And you have ice cream on your nose."

Carly giggled.

"Here, let me get that," Beth said. She wiped Carly's face. As Carly took another lick, ice cream again went everywhere.

Quinton and Beth exchanged a look, and Beth rolled her eyes. He laughed. "We'll clean her up before we get back on the road," he said.

Carly fell asleep a little after eight. After her incessant talk about trying on her flower girl dress abruptly ended and one or two light snores were heard, she gave one last sigh and succumbed to deep sleep.

"Is it always like that?" Quinton asked.

Beth swiveled her head but could see only his profile in the darkened interior of the sedan. "Like what?"

"Going strong and then suddenly nothing."

"Sometimes. It's like whatever little battery she has suddenly runs out. Trust me, though. She'll be recharged by tomorrow morning. I'm just hoping her endless energy doesn't give your mother fits or aggravate her heart condition."

"It'll be fine," Quinton said. "She did raise two children. She'll get back in the swing of it. Isn't it like riding a bike? You never forget?"

"As I'm still riding the parenting bike, I don't have a clue about it," Beth said. "Maybe it's easier the second time around. You know what to do, having already experienced it all."

"Perhaps," Quinton said. "Even though my classes provide hands-on experience with kids, medical school didn't teach me the emotions that go along with parenting. When Carly put her hand in mine tonight…"

His voice trailed off. A mile seemed to fly by before he spoke again. Lights from a billboard advertising a hotel chain suddenly illuminated Quinton's profile.

"I owe you an apology," he finally said. "I have all this book knowledge but no real parenting experience. Heck, I haven't even decided if I want my own kids. I doubt I'd be any good as a parent. But that's beside the point. When she put her hand in mine, I truly understood what being trusted means. You'd do anything for her, wouldn't you?"

"Yes," Beth said. She let the word hang in the air.

"I called you a bad parent. I was wrong."

After his apology, he gripped the steering wheel tighter. She suddenly realized she was twisting the hem of her turtleneck. She released it.

"Don't worry about it," she said. "We all make mistakes. You don't want to know what I thought about you."

Quinton chuckled, a deep sound that filled the sedan. "No, I probably don't, but I'm sure I deserved it."

"Oh, you did," Beth confirmed. "At the time."

"So you can forgive me?"

"I already have," Beth said, using the words she often used with her daughter. To forgive Quinton was easy if she didn't consider him anything more than a friend or a business colleague. Besides, she reminded herself, he wasn't her type any more than she was his. And there were worse things than being alone.

She shook her head and used the lull to say, "This radio station's about gone. Do you mind if I find another one?"

"No," Quinton said. He gestured to the radio. "You don't even have to ask. You can change it whenever. I may have some CDs in the glove compartment. I'm not too particular about what I listen to."

"But you might have been listening to the song," Beth said. "I couldn't just change it."

He glanced at her. "Why not?"

Beth leaned forward and pressed the scan button. "I guess I'm not used to that. Randy controlled the radio in our house. He drove, so he said he got to choose."

"Tell me about him," Quinton said.

"There's not much to tell," Beth said. "We were two people who probably shouldn't have gotten married. I'm the one who insisted. We had a child on the way. Although she wasn't supposed to happen, that child back there is the best thing in my life. She's never been a mistake."

"Of course she isn't. She's a gem, and it's obvious to anyone who looks at you how much you adore her," Quinton said.

Beth heard the conviction in his voice. "She's my whole world," she said.

The tires hummed as Quinton braked and took the exit ramp. He turned left and pulled into a gas station. "Do you need anything? Water? Soda?"

"Just the facilities and a brief leg stretch," Beth said. She peeked into the back seat. Carly remained sound asleep. "Do me a favor and keep an eye on Carly. If she wakes up, I'll have to take her in with me. We don't want any accidents or unscheduled pit stops."

"We're making pretty good time, so that sounds good," Quinton said. "If you don't want anything, I'll just pay at the pump."

He drew his coat around him and pulled on his leather gloves before exiting the car. The wind had gotten sharper, and the air felt like impending snow, although snow wasn't in the weather forecast.

"It's cold," Beth said before walking quickly toward the store. Within seconds, she'd disappeared inside.

Quinton began the pump, set the automatic shutoff and slid back into the car. He gave a shiver as his body readjusted to shelter from the elements. A small sigh came from the back seat, and he turned around.

Carly's head had tilted to one side, almost resting on her shoulder. To an adult, the position would be torture, but Carly didn't appear to notice. Her tiny chest rose and fell in rhythmic breathing. The blanket she never was without had slipped from her hands and onto the seat beside her. Quinton he went to grab it, but then he resisted the urge. His movement might wake her and that wouldn't be good.

So in the lights and shadows from the gas station, Quinton simply watched Carly sleep. Her usually expressive little face had relaxed into flawless porcelain. Her lips were curved into a smile. Quinton inhaled sharply. He'd seen sleeping children before, but with Carly…was this what gazing on an angel was like?

He shifted forward to stare out the front windshield at the darkened countryside surrounding the gas station. The unknown was out there. It shouldn't be in the car with him. He was Dr. Quinton Searle, the man with the plan. He knew what he wanted, and how to get it. His life was great, and would be even better once he got his parents off his case.

But the unknown *had* crept in somehow when he hadn't been expecting it. Strange feelings were flowing through him, as if filling a hole in his life that he hadn't realized existed.

When Carly had put her hand in his earlier and hugged him right as they'd gotten ice cream—

The pump clicked, mercifully signaling that the gas tank was full and that he had a job to do. Jobs were good. They gave a man a purpose, a reason to avoid thinking. Quinton stepped out of the car and braved the cold again.

"Done?" Beth asked as she came back.

"Yeah, but I'm going to go inside and get some coffee," he said. "Are you sure you don't want anything?"

Beth shook her head. "No. I don't want us to have to stop again if we don't need to."

"We won't," Quinton said. "We've only got about

two hours, tops. Be right back." Within a few minutes they were back on the road.

Two hours later Beth discovered that Quinton had been right about the time. Once over the Mississippi River, they would be in St. Louis.

"I've never seen this skyline," Beth said. "It's beautiful. All those tall buildings light up the Arch. What bridge is over there?"

"Eads," Quinton said. They drove onto the Poplar Street Bridge and the Arch and Eads Bridge were now to Beth's right. "There's a city ordinance or something prohibiting buildings from being taller than the Arch. But they might seem taller because they're on higher ground."

"Oh," Beth said, her gaze now on Busch Stadium. She recognized the familiar landmark from television. Beth was a Chicago Cubs fan. Despite being tired, she found herself wide-awake as Quinton narrated their journey to his childhood home. He pointed out Forest Park, with its Science Center and the St. Louis Zoo; then they passed the St. Louis Galleria—"Only one of the places my mother haunts"—before he finally exited the interstate at McKnight Road. He drove only a bit, then veered left onto a new road. The houses seemed to get larger and larger and farther and farther apart.

"Oh, God," she whispered. Did that house have three stories? And for how many people? These houses were bigger than some of the houses in Chicago, even that one in the movie *Home Alone,* which had been huge.

"Did you say something?" Quinton said. He turned the radio off, then glanced at her. "Is something wrong?"

"I was just looking at these houses," Beth said.

"This is Ladue," Quinton said. "Can you picture me living here?" Beth didn't have a chance to answer as Quinton said, "Oh, great."

This was her chance to ask "What's wrong?"

He pointed to a house still some distance off. Even from where they were, Beth could see that the massive house had light pouring from every window.

"That's it," Quinton said. "And so much for a 'sneaky, we'll-meet-everyone-tomorrow' entry."

The clock on the radio indicated it was nearing one a.m. They pulled into a driveway that led to a four-car garage. Panic fluttered through Beth. Just how many people were here? And… "Everyone's still awake?"

Quinton killed the engine and turned to her. "Oh, they're definitely still awake. All of them and waiting to greet my fiancée enthusiastically."

"You're kidding, right?"

The front door opened and light spilled out onto the circular driveway.

"Leave the stuff," Quinton said. "We can get it later. We'd better face everyone."

"Okay," Beth said. The night had turned bitterly cold, and she zipped her coat all the way up to her chin before climbing out of the car. Within moments Beth had Carly in her arms. She put a heavy blanket over

Carly's face, then followed Quinton up the stairs and into the foyer. Beth blinked as the bright interior lights hit her eyes.

"Thank goodness you're finally here!" Babs said. "We've been worried that you would never arrive, and the wind is getting so nasty."

"How was the drive? Flying would have been faster."

This question came from a gentleman Beth assumed to be Quinton's father, but she wasn't sure. There were two elderly men standing inside the doorway.

"Close the door. All the cold air is getting in," Babs said.

After Quinton closed the door, Beth removed the blanket from Carly's face.

"I'm Uncle Bob! Nice to meet you!"

Beth suddenly found herself trying to shake hands with a portly but stylishly attired man in his mid-fifties. "This is my wife, Joan."

"Hello," Beth said. So the other man had been Quinton's father.

She shifted Carly to her other arm and looked at Quinton for help. Didn't he understand? She had to get Carly to safety or…it was no use.

Her sleeping angel blinked once and said, "Mommy, where are we?"

"Why, where Quinton grew up," Babs said. She touched the pearls at her neck as if shocked that Carly didn't know.

"Go back to sleep, angel," Beth said.

"I'm hungry," Carly said. She blinked again and glanced around the room. "Mommy, who are all these people?"

"Quinton's family," Beth said. "You can meet them in the morning."

"Hungry," Carly repeated. She clutched her blanket.

Beth shot Quinton an exasperated expression. "I need to feed her and get her back to bed," she said.

"Okay," he said. "Mom, where are Beth and Carly sleeping? Is Carly in the nursery?"

"No nursery. Not tired," Carly insisted. "I'm hungry. Want food."

"We have tons of leftovers in the kitchen," Babs said. "The caterer left salmon, chicken and—"

"Peanut butter and jelly will do fine," Beth said quickly. "Really, the simpler the better right now."

Babs frowned. "I think we may have those items. I'm not sure. I guess we'll find out. Follow me."

As Babs led Beth into the huge kitchen, Beth couldn't help but stare. Complete with two built-in Subzero refrigerators and two Dacor stoves, the kitchen was a cook's dream. However, Babs couldn't cook, a fact she admitted after she wasn't able to locate the peanut butter. "I use caterers," she said, "and the housekeeper prepares meals, as well."

"Hungry," Carly repeated. She wiggled in Beth's arms.

"Shh," Beth said. "In a minute. I'm sure there is something."

"Let me," Quinton said as he appeared in the

kitchen. He grinned at Carly and tapped her nose with his fingertip. "I bet you I can find you something to eat."

Carly giggled.

"You haven't lived here in ages," Babs said.

"No, but unlike you, my dear mother, I know how to forage." Within seconds, Quinton had managed to discover a loaf of bread and a container of peanut butter. The only spread, though, was an orange marmalade.

"I hate orange," Carly said. "Yuck."

"Then it's a plain peanut butter sandwich for you," Beth said. Carly was heavy, and Beth's arms were tiring from holding her.

"We have shrimp, some fried morels, some pesto and some spinach dip with wheat wafers," Babs said helpfully. "I know where all that is."

Quinton opened the doors to one of the refrigerators, and Beth heard a plastic bag rustling.

"What about chicken?" he called. "Do you like chicken strips, Carly? They're like chicken nuggets, only with a long shape, instead."

Carly nodded. "I like chicken," she said. "With ketchup."

Quinton removed the package of chicken from the refrigerator.

Babs frowned as she saw the plastic package. "Where did that come from?" she asked.

"It seems Dad has been stopping at Schnucks for his late-night snacks," Quinton said. He opened the bag and took out a cold chicken strip, tore off a portion of the tender and put it in his mouth. "Pretty good stuff." He swallowed. "How does she like it? Hot or cold?"

"Heated," Beth said.

Quinton's sister wandered into the kitchen and watched as Quinton located a plate, placed the chicken tenders on it and microwaved the lot.

"Go ahead and set Carly over there," Quinton said, noticing Beth still held her daughter.

Beth sat Carly on a chair at the granite kitchen table. She took off Carly's coat and draped it over another chair, then followed with hers.

"So when did you get so handy?" Shelby asked her brother.

"I've lived on my own since I left here," Quinton said. "That was almost eighteen years ago."

"I thought doctors just ate in the hospital cafeteria," she said.

"Your dad eats here," her mother pointed out.

"But he doesn't cook," Shelby said. "Marni does it. You sure don't."

"True," Babs acknowledged.

The microwave beeped and Quinton removed the chicken. He placed the food in front of Carly, then found the ketchup and squirted a generous portion onto the plate. "Watch out—it might be hot," he warned.

"Okay." Carly picked up a tender, blew on it a few times, dipped it in ketchup, then stuck it in her mouth. She nodded as she chewed. "Good."

"Don't speak with your mouth full," Beth said. She

glanced up at Quinton. "Could I trouble you for some water?"

He grinned. "Of course. Would you like it with ice?"

"It's for Carly," she said.

"I'll get you some, too," he replied. Within seconds, he'd brought back two glasses of ice water. "Drink up. You need to stay hydrated. I don't want you getting sick again."

She didn't want to be sick again, either, for that would mean depending on Quinton more, but Beth simply accepted it and said, "Thanks." She drank most of the water. She hadn't had anything since dinner and she was thirsty.

"I can't believe how domestic you are," Shelby said. "Beth, have you worked this miracle on my brother?"

"Really, no," Beth said.

"Of course she has," Quinton replied.

He rested his hand on Beth's shoulder. As a heat traveled through her, she tried not to squirm. She was supposed to be the doting fiancée. They should act loving. And it wasn't as if his touch wasn't welcome. Oh, no, that was the problem. Her body was reacting to him. Dear Lord. She *could not* want this man.

"She's the best thing that's happened to me," Quinton said.

Which of course wasn't true, Beth thought as she plastered an adoring smile on her face. She wasn't even his type. Her body might like his touch—okay, even welcome it—but she had to stand firm. She was not the best thing that had happened to him. She was just a way for him to get his family off his case.

"Really," Quinton said. "My life has taken a turn for the better since I met Beth."

"Oh, that's so sweet," Shelby said. "I never knew you were such a romantic." She sniffed suddenly as tears welled up in her eyes.

"Hey, what's wrong? What did I say? You look like you're going to cry," Quinton said.

"It's not you," Shelby said. "You are so sweet and romantic. It's me. Hormones."

"Shelby!" Babs's tone contained a stern warning.

"Oh, I know it's supposed to be a secret until after the wedding, but he's my brother. Quinton, guess what? I'm pregnant!"

"Shelby!" This time Babs shrieked.

"Oh, Mom, Quinton's a doctor and my brother. Besides, no one cares in this day and age," Shelby said. She dabbed her eyes. "I'm a lawyer, for goodness' sake, not a tramp. And Alan and I have been living together for a year. So what if I'm having a baby?"

Carly knew that word. "Who's having a baby?" she asked.

"Aunt Shelby," Quinton replied. "Congratulations."

"I was a baby," Carly said. "I was in my mommy's tummy once."

"You were," Beth said.

Carly stared at Shelby. "Your tummy isn't very big."

Shelby laughed and again became teary eyed. She situated her hands on her stomach. "No, but it will be soon. Can you believe it, Quinton? I'm going to have a baby."

"She just found out two days ago," Babs said, as if that explained Shelby's erratic behavior.

Shelby smiled at everyone as she shared her happiness. "So when are you two going to add another one? You want a little brother or sister, don't you, Carly?"

"There's no baby in my mommy's tummy," Carly said. "I'm out."

"No, but there may be after your mommy and Quinton get married," Shelby said.

Carly's forehead furrowed as she tried to make sense of what Shelby had said. Carly's last chicken tender lay forgotten in the remnants of the ketchup. "If Quinton and my mommy have a baby, that means I'll have a brother or sister."

"Right," Shelby said.

"So Quinton will be the baby's daddy."

"Right," Shelby said again. "That's because your mommy and Quinton are getting married. Married people can have babies."

Carly swiveled in her chair so that she could peer at Quinton. She stared at him, and he shifted as though under a hot spotlight. "Quinton, if you and Mommy are going to be married and have a baby…are you going to be my daddy, too?"

As QUINTON WONDERED what to say, his father entered the room. Quinton had never been so happy to see Fred Searle in his life.

"Why are we all hiding out in here?" his father

boomed. "Hey, Quinton, it's starting to snow. You might want to bring in your luggage."

"I thought it wasn't supposed to snow," Babs said.

"You know those weathermen. They're always wrong," Fred said. "They say no accumulation—we get six inches. It better not snow. The game's tomorrow."

"I'll go get the bags," Quinton said.

"I'll help," Beth said. She grabbed her coat. "Carly, you'll be okay here. Finish your last piece of chicken."

"Fred can assist Quinton with the bags," Babs said.

"No, really," Beth said. "I'll go."

"Loved ones want to be alone," Fred said. "So, Carly, I see you found my chicken fingers. Did you save me some?"

"There are a few left in the fridge," Quinton called back over his shoulder. "I hid them behind the milk."

"Thanks."

Quinton stopped in the hall and waited until Beth was right behind him. "Don't worry, they can't harm her."

"She's already been harmed," Beth hissed as he helped her into her coat. "She thinks you're going to be her dad!"

She waited only until the thick front door was shut behind them before saying, "This has gone too far, Quinton! My daughter can't believe that you will be her father. She's already lost one. What am I going to do? She can't lose another person in her life. We have to end this now. Let's go back in there and tell them that this is a charade. That this isn't real. That this isn't—"

Quinton silenced her the only way he knew how. He brought his lips down on hers.

Chapter Seven

The only thing that registered in Beth's brain was how good Quinton's lips felt on hers. Gone was the cold air, the lightly falling snow. In their place was a heat unlike anything she'd ever experienced previously in her life.

While Quinton had certainly kissed her before, he hadn't kissed her like this. This kiss demanded. This kiss asked to be kissed in return. This kiss took her breath away. Literally.

She sighed into him, her argument left unspoken and temporarily forgotten as his tongue mated with hers. For when he kissed her, she really couldn't think of anything she wanted to say. Kissing Quinton was like sinking into a warm bath. Decadent. Delicious. Divine.

Long pent-up desire swept through Beth, and as Quinton's arms drew her closer to him, she succumbed further into the delirium racing through her as he deepened the kiss.

"Oh, good. I thought you two were fighting or something. You just wanted to kiss. I know how that is. Anyway, you both are going to turn into Popsicles if you stay out here longer, and Carly says she's tired." Shelby's voice intruded into the magical moment, and Beth stumbled as she freed herself from Quinton's arms.

"Steady," he said. He reached out to cup her elbow, but Beth sidestepped him.

Steady? After that kiss Beth doubted she'd ever be steady on her feet again. He'd shattered every bit of her precarious control over the situation. Worse, every kiss she'd ever had before this one now paled in comparison. Maybe it was because she'd been without a man for a long time. Plus, after a while Randy hadn't wanted her much, and then he'd been ill, and…

No, that wasn't it. The passion she'd felt with Quinton wasn't desperation or lack of physical contact. It was because her body fit Quinton's like a glove. Her body molded to his as if she'd been made for him. The thought unsettled her equilibrium and she stood there as he grabbed their things.

"I've got everything," Quinton said. His breath appeared as a white cloud in front of him. "It's cold. Let's go in. We can talk inside."

Beth didn't answer him but instead headed into the house. Shelby stood just inside the front door. "Carly was starting to fall asleep at the table. I didn't mean to interrupt anything."

That sounded like her daughter. "Her adrenaline

must have worn off. She's usually a sound sleeper. What bedroom are we going to be in?"

"Mom has a bedroom just for her," Quinton said. "The old nursery."

"She can sleep with me," Beth offered.

"That's not really necessary," Babs said as she appeared in the hall. "Shelby's old nursery room is still filled with stuffed animals, dolls, and it's painted a delightful shade of pink. I never had the heart to have it changed. I knew I'd have granddaughters someday. It'll be right next door to your bedroom."

"If it's right next door—" Beth began.

"Oh, it is," Babs said. "And Fred already took her upstairs. He has such a way with children. That's why his practice thrives so much. Quinton follows right in his footsteps. Follow me, I'll show you where everything is. And Shelby, shut that door behind your brother. I swear, we always seem to be heating the outdoors."

Shelby rolled her eyes and gave Beth a conspiratorial smile before Beth turned and followed Babs up the main staircase. Beth's rubber-soled tennis shoes made little sound on the marble steps. She reached the second floor landing.

"It's right down here," Babs said as she turned down another hallway. "You'll be in this room, and right here, this is Carly's."

Babs paused in the hall just outside the door. As Beth approached, she heard Fred Searle's voice. "And then the last little piggy said wee wee wee and ran all the way home."

Carly giggled. "What then?" Beth heard her daughter ask.

"Why, the piggies all went to bed."

Beth entered the ten by ten room just in time to see Carly's eyes widen as she said, "They did?"

"They did." Fred said with a solemn nod. "Just like you need to do. In fact, here's your mommy now to kiss you good-night. She's going to be right next door, although what did we turn on to keep any bad dreams away?"

"Bedtime butterfly!" Carly announced. She pointed to a pink butterfly shaped night-light that sat on the white dresser. The pink-and-white room was every little girl's fantasy.

"And you have your blanket, too."

"I do," Carly said. She clutched it to her.

"Then I'll leave you so your mommy can kiss you good-night. You sleep well." From where he'd been sitting on the edge of the bed, Fred rose to his feet. "All yours," he told Beth as he passed.

"Thanks," she said. She went to sit next to Carly. "Hi, angel. Sleepy now that you've eaten?"

"Uh-huh," Carly said. "And Grandpa showed me the piggy game."

Grandpa. A chill went through Beth. "He did, huh?"

"Yep. And the piggies went home to sleep, just like I'm going to do. Tomorrow Grandpa said I can play with the dolls and the stuffies."

"You can," Beth said. She leaned over and kissed Carly's forehead. "Close your eyes, darling. I'll be nearby."

"I'm not afraid," Carly said. "This is where my new daddy grew up. He *is* going to be my new daddy, right?"

Beth's heart constricted. "Shh. We'll talk in the morning. It's almost two a.m. You need to get some sleep before the sun comes up."

"Okay," Carly said. "'Night."

Beth stroked Carly's forehead and Carly closed her eyes. Within a moment Carly's breathing became regular, and Beth knew her daughter was asleep.

"She's a sweetheart, isn't she?" Quinton stood inside the doorway, lowering Carly's small suitcase. "You can unpack this tomorrow. Let's get you settled in."

"Okay," Beth said. Suddenly she was tired, both physically and mentally. Only a short while ago, she'd almost become homeless. Now she was figuratively homeless. Her life wasn't her own but rather one big lie.

The room Quinton led her to was about fourteen feet square and came complete with a canopied queen-size bed. Beth knew enough about furniture to recognize the style of the rest of the pieces as Queen Anne. "This is lovely," Beth said.

"Good, because it's yours until Sunday." He set her carry-on suitcase on the dresser. "Feel free to use the drawers and closet. This is a guest bedroom, so you won't be intruding."

"Thanks," she said. She plopped down on the bed.

"You look exhausted," he observed.

"Very," she admitted.

He studied her for a moment. "All this is getting to you, isn't it?"

"I don't want to fight," Beth said. "I just want this to be over so that we can go back to our own lives."

"We have this weekend and next," he said.

"I can't wait," Beth replied. She reached down and began to unlace her tennis shoes. "I need my life back. I need to get everything stable again."

"I understand," Quinton said, coming over to sit beside her. He lifted her legs and pulled them onto his lap. With gentle but firm hands he began to massage her feet through her socks.

"That feels heavenly," Beth said.

"It's supposed to," Quinton replied. "Just relax and enjoy it. That shouldn't be too hard to do."

"Actually, it *is* hard to relax around you," Beth admitted.

"Really?" Quinton moved his attention to her other foot. "You aren't relaxing right now?"

Beth leaned back against the pillow shams. "Okay, right now I am."

"So when don't you relax? You recovered at my place. You mean you really don't relax?"

"Really," Beth replied. Sleep started to tiptoe around the edges of her eyelids. "I can't relax around you. I have to keep up my guard. I have a child who wants this fantasy. I can't let it go too far. I have to move out eventually, and when you do nice things like this, you're making it hard for me to want to leave—

but leave I must. And you certainly can't kiss me again."

"But what if I want to kiss you again? What if I liked it?" There was a huskiness in his voice.

"You can't," Beth said. She closed her eyes. He was working such magic on her aching feet.

"You didn't like me kissing you?"

"Maybe I like it too much. It makes me believe things I shouldn't. I'm too old for fairy tales. We're a business partnership. At the end, I have to go."

"Well, maybe I don't want you to go. I'm kind of getting used to having you and Carly around. I didn't realize the apartment was so big and lonely until you moved into it."

"We're just saving you from your family." The pillow underneath Beth's head felt really soft. "We're not your type."

"Now, why would you say that?"

But Beth couldn't reply. Exhaustion had claimed her voice and her thoughts. She could hear and feel, though.

Quinton lifted her legs and moved her onto the bed. She felt him remove her socks and shift her so that he could cover her with the down comforter. He loosened her belt and the button of her jeans, but there his fingers stopped.

He pressed his warm lips on her forehead. "Sleep well, sweetheart," he said.

Then his lips were on hers. It was a gentle kiss, designed only to be feathery and then lift away. But Beth started and her eyes flew open. She stared into Quinton's eyes.

"I like kissing you," he said. "I think we should explore this chemistry we have between us."

"It's only chemistry," Beth said. She managed to say the words, but beneath the comforter her body trembled.

"Maybe," Quinton said. His gray eyes darkened. "But we should explore it. Chemistry is rare, you know."

"Is it?"

"It is." He leaned down and kissed her lightly. Then he drew back with a groan. "We will explore what's going on between us," he said. "But not tonight. Tonight I want you to rest."

His fingertips were gentle as he pressed her eyelids closed. As soon as the darkness seeped in, sleep began to claim her.

"There. Those blues of yours were too tempting. Rest up, and I'll see you in the morning."

"Okay," Beth mumbled. The she turned her head and slept.

Quinton watched for a moment before clicking off the light beside her bed. Semidarkness filled the room, the only light coming from the hallway. How fitting, Quinton thought. She resided in the shadows, a mysterious and illusive figure he couldn't figure out.

But he wanted to figure her out. Soon.

BETH SLEPT IN until ten. Once up, she and Quinton took Carly to the Magic House in Kirkwood. That evening she and Quinton accompanied his dad to a St. Louis University basketball game.

"I went to SLU," Fred said as he waved a big blue hand emblazoned with #1 Billikens on it. Everyone on the stands wore blue and white. "Haven't missed a game that I've had tickets to in the past twenty years."

"This is his thing," Quinton, on Beth's left, leaned over and whispered in her ear. "We're honored guests, so I hope you're having fun."

Beth nodded. "It's great," she said.

"Why didn't you go here?" she asked suddenly as the thought entered her head. "They have a medical school, don't they?"

Quinton looked down at the court, his expression clouded. "I wanted to get out of St. Louis."

"Ah," Beth said.

Quinton cheered as the Billikens took possession of the ball and ran it downcourt for a basket. "I've been to just about every one of these games with him. Mom doesn't like to go. She's not really the sports type," he said.

Now that she'd met his mother, Beth understood why Babs wasn't in attendance. Instead, she'd insisted on keeping Carly with her, trying on Carly's flower girl dress and working on Carly's posture for the wedding. Beth hadn't wanted to leave her daughter, but it was Babs's anniversary weekend.

There was a brief lull as halftime began. Quinton's dad went to greet some friends, leaving Quinton and Beth alone in the Savvis Center stands.

"Are you sure I can't get you anything? More nachos? Soda?"

"Stop fussing over me," Beth said. "I don't need a thing. I'm fine."

"If you're sure," he said. He rubbed his hands before reaching for hers. "I worry about you," he said.

"Well, stop. You don't need to worry. I've been taking care of myself for a long time. I'm pretty good at it."

"That's why you fainted in my arms," he said.

"I wouldn't have if you hadn't cost me money," Beth retorted.

"But then we wouldn't be where we are today," he said.

"Which is nowhere," Beth insisted. "Okay, maybe we are somewhere. We're at a college basketball game, cheering for your dad's alma mater."

Quinton grinned at her. "Do you know what I want right now?"

Her forehead furrowed and her skin prickled. Why was he staring at her like that? "Uh, no."

"I'd like to kiss you again," Quinton said.

The halftime show started on the court, but Beth didn't notice. At his words, an illicit thrill shot through her. Hadn't she wanted Quinton to notice her that night? Hadn't she wanted just a little ego massage? Oh, he was laying it on now, wasn't he?

"You can't," she said, trying to make light of the moment. "We're in public."

"So?" His voice had a sexual edge, and offered a challenge that was hard to resist.

But Beth tried. "PDA. Public display of affection. Bad example to the surrounding community, and besides, your dad will be right back."

"So?" Quinton said. He leaned forward slightly, his nose almost touching hers.

"So..." Beth faltered as the truth hit her. She *wanted* him to kiss her. She wanted his lips on hers, wanted the fire that she'd felt the night before, the fire that she'd thought had been forever extinguished inside her. All she had to do was tilt her face up.

"Did I miss anything?"

"No," Beth said as Fred returned, saving her from her moment of truth. She ducked her head out of reach of Quinton's lips, stepped away and said, "Nothing's happened yet."

"Quinton, I think I like this girl," Fred said. "You did well, son. You did well."

"I think so," Quinton said.

Beth turned to watch the show. Maybe she should send him out for something to drink. Quinton couldn't like her. He was acting. That was all it was. Acting and chemistry.

And chemistry had gotten her into trouble before. A lot of trouble.

The Billikens won, and Fred, Quinton and Beth arrived back at the house late. Beth checked on Carly, and barely made it into bed it seemed before she was up the next day for the anniversary brunch. Since Shelby and her fiancé had a couples' shower that night, Babs and Fred were celebrating their anniversary with family.

They also had a trip scheduled for March. "After all," Babs had told Beth, "I've been married a long time and my daughter comes first."

Thus, at the ends of the table were Babs and Fred, and surrounding them were Uncle Bob and Aunt Joan; Carly; Quinton; Beth; Shelby; her fiancé, Alan; his parents and his sister.

"So have you set a date?" Joan asked, interrupting Beth's thoughts. "Back-to-back weddings, Babs. You must be thrilled."

"Oh, I am," Babs said.

"We haven't set a date," Quinton said. "We were considering a long engagement."

"Long engagements are so boring," Joan replied. "And neither of you is getting any younger. You'll want to start your family soon."

"I practiced being a flower girl yesterday," Carly said.

"And you did a very good job," Babs said. "You should have seen her, Evelyn. She'll be perfect."

"That's good," Evelyn said.

Beth sensed that Evelyn hadn't liked the addition to the wedding party. "I did receive confirmation that you ordered your tux, Quinton."

"I said I would," he replied. "I have a busy schedule, but I got it done. The tailor said he had plenty of time."

Evelyn ignored that, instead putting a forkful of stuffing into her mouth.

"I just can't believe we'll be married in only a little

over a week." Shelby placed her hand on Alan's and suddenly looked ready to cry.

When he said "I know," she did cry.

"Oh, it's the hormones again," Babs said.

"Beth, did you have happy-crying hormones when you were pregnant?" Shelby asked as she dabbed her eyes with the cloth napkin. Alan was handing her a glass of water.

There had been nothing happy about the early stages of her pregnancy. She and Randy had fought constantly, first over her refusal to have an abortion, then over her insistence that he do the right thing and marry her. "No," Beth replied. "But they're common. They mean you'll have an easy pregnancy."

Her little white lie—Beth had made all that up— helped, though, for Shelby brightened. "Oh, good," she said. "I'd love an easy pregnancy. I've heard that labor can be hard."

"Shelby, not at the dinner table. You and Beth can talk later about that," Babs said.

"You're right," Shelby said. "I just heard also that my fingers will swell and I won't be able to wear my rings." She toyed with her engagement ring for a second, then looked up. "Which reminds me. I haven't seen yours, Beth. You didn't have it last time. Hold out your hand and let me take a look at your engagement ring."

And at that moment, time seemed to freeze. She'd gone back to work, and neither she nor Quinton had given getting a fake ring for a fake engagement a second thought.

"Come on," Evelyn coaxed.

"You did get her a ring, didn't you?" Babs asked.

Beth yanked her hand under the table. "It's still being resized," she said.

"Well, this just won't do." Babs appeared totally affronted. She fanned herself slightly with her hand as if the room had suddenly gotten hotter. "We have Alan and Shelby's couples' shower tonight. We just cannot keep saying to people that the ring is getting resized. That simply won't do."

"It's tacky," Evelyn agreed. "Couldn't the jeweler have gotten it done? This must be some ring for it to be taking this long."

There was no ring, but of course neither Quinton nor Beth could admit that.

"Really, it's not a big deal," Quinton began, but Babs's expression silenced him.

"It is a gross gaffe," Babs said. She looked down the table at her husband. "Wouldn't you agree, Fred?"

"I would agree," Evelyn said before Fred could say anything. "Without a ring, who can tell if you're really serious?"

"Oh, Quinton's serious," Shelby said. "He's never had a girl here in St. Louis past high school. And Beth and Carly are living with him."

Babs fanned herself with her linen napkin. "All the more reason to have something on her finger. We don't need the gossip."

"Mom, no one cares," Shelby said. "It's like with the baby and—"

"I care," Babs said, and Beth knew from Babs's tone that that would be that on this topic. "We'll just have to find a ring that can work for this weekend." She glanced at Beth's hand. "I know. I have Fred's mother's wedding ring upstairs in the safe. It's a simple solitaire, it should be perfect. I'll go get it."

Babs stood up and left the room.

"She won't mind?" Evelyn asked.

Bob and Joan appeared mystified by the whole situation. Everyone turned to gaze at Fred Searle. He took a long sip of water before speaking.

"My mother's been gone about twenty years now," Fred answered. "She won't mind at all. In fact, she'd probably be delighted that someone is getting some use out of the ring. The only reason we didn't bury her in that ring is that my dad bought her a larger diamond on their tenth anniversary, after they'd become financially successful. She wore that ring, instead, because it showed he would marry her all over again."

"That story always makes me cry," Shelby said, breaking into another round of tears. Alan offered her his dinner napkin.

Babs came back with a threadbare velvet ring box. "This is it," she said, handing the black box to Beth.

Beth stared at the box, which fit squarely in the palm of her right hand. She lifted the lid. Inside the box was the most gorgeous diamond ring she'd ever seen.

"Now, it's a small solitaire, but remarkably clear and well cut," Babs said. "Just mention it's an heirloom and everyone will understand."

Beth glanced up and realized that Babs was serious. She kept her response of "Why would anyone care?" to herself. The ring was beautiful; she hadn't even had an engagement ring from Randy. And her gold wedding band had been plain, simple and maybe $375 at the most.

The ring she now held had a history of love behind it, which made the heirloom more precious than a more expensive diamond. Beth closed the box.

"I can't wear this," she said.

Babs frowned. "Of course you can," she insisted. "Keep the ring until yours is sized. Better yet, just keep it. I'm sure Edna would not mind you having it. In fact, she probably would have liked you a great deal. Lord knows she certainly didn't approve of me. No one was good enough for her little boy."

"She was always too tough on you," Joan said in defense of her sister.

"But Babs is right. My mother would have liked you," Fred said with a smile. "So take the ring and put it on. Let's see how it fits."

"Hopefully it won't need resizing," Evelyn said.

Beth's left hand shook as she opened the box again. She set the box on the table and lifted the ring out of it. The diamond glittered, reflecting the lights of the chandelier.

"Really, I…" Beth began. "This is all too…"

Warm fingers covered her own. "Let me," Quinton said. He took the ring out of her grasp and turned her left hand toward his. Beth's heart stopped as he slid the ring onto her finger. It fit perfectly, as somehow she'd known it would. She stared at the ring, too afraid to glance up and discover what emotions might be on Quinton's face.

"Perfect," Babs pronounced. "Excellent. That problem's solved."

"Me see," Carly said. Beth swiveled to her right and held out her left hand. "Pretty," Carly said. "I want a ring."

"When you're older," Babs said.

Three hours passed before Beth got Quinton alone. They were standing in the upstairs hallway, having finally put Carly to sleep way past her naptime. The guests had vanished, Babs had gone shopping and Fred was snoring in his favorite easy chair in the family room. Beth followed Quinton to his room.

"I can't wear this ring," she said.

He looked surprised. "Why? Doesn't it fit?"

"It fits, but *we* don't fit. We aren't real, Quinton, but this ring is. If something happens to this ring, I can't afford to replace it."

Quinton shrugged. "My grandmother's been gone for a long time, so it's not a big deal," he said. "And I'm sure my mother has it insured. So don't worry about it."

He simply didn't understand. Beth tried again. She waved her hand. "This is all a charade."

"Your wearing that ring makes my mother happy. So do it. It's a role you agreed to play, a role you took on after you'd told me you weren't going to."

Those were fighting words. Randy had always said the same thing. "*You* insisted we get married. *You* insisted on having this baby. *You* insisted…"

Quinton had just changed the word *insist* to *agreed* and *started*.

Beth sighed and let her anger go. She wasn't going to fight Quinton. She was tired of fighting; it had gotten her nowhere in life except having to eke out an existence. And in a few weeks, she'd be out of Quinton's life for good. Letting him have his way rather than make him understand would be easier.

"Fine," Beth said.

He sensed her withdrawal, her change in attitude. "What's wrong?" he said.

"Nothing's wrong. You win this round. I'm not going to get into a verbal sparring match with you. You're right. I told your mother we were engaged. I can play this role I created a little while longer, and then it'll be all over. They'll leave you alone, I'll be on my feet and both our lives will go on as before."

Quinton stared locked gazes with her. He put a finger under her chin and lifted her face. "Who hurt you, Beth?" Quinton asked. "Who did a number on you?"

"No one did a number on me, Quinton. I'm tired, this is all very stressful and I'm ready to go home, although I don't have a home to go to."

His expression was dubious. "Let my place be your home."

"No, I can't," Beth said. "And I really don't know why you want me or—"

"I want you because you're you," Quinton said. "Do you know how much I want to make love to you?"

His words immediately made her body respond. She wanted to make love to him, too. She wanted to feel him skin to skin, to experience the chemistry that had been ebbing and flowing between them ever since she'd met him. She pushed doubts and her conscience aside.

Right now she wanted passion and everything that came with it. If only for a moment. If only to remind herself what it was like to be a woman in love with a man.

In love?

She didn't have time to contemplate those words, for Quinton's lips were already on hers.

"I want you," he told her again between kisses. He pushed the door to his bedroom open and guided her in. She heard the door click shut behind her. Only his voice was audible in the twilight.

"Let me make love to you, Beth."

He made no promises, spoke no other words. He just took her silence and clinging mouth as acceptance. She pressed herself to him—a moth to a flame. No, not a moth, Beth thought as his lips found the hollow at the base of her neck. A moth had no choice in being drawn to a flame. She had a choice. She could say no and Quinton would stop. He was a gentleman; he would never hurt her or force her to do something she didn't want to do. He wouldn't press or ask her why. He would simply stop.

But stopping wasn't an option. She'd been without a man's touch for too long, but then, Quinton was no ordinary man. She needed him, and only him.

As his fingers found the vee of her shirt, she leaned back to allow him access. When he bent his head to kiss the valley between her breasts, she gasped and a shiver shot through her. Having this man, being one with him, if only for today, was as essential as breathing.

He laid her tenderly on the bed and soon joined her. He'd shed his shirt, a presumption Beth didn't mind as she touched his chest. His workouts had paid off, and she splayed her fingers over smooth, hard muscles that felt wonderful under her touch. His skin warmed where she stroked it. He gave a groan and claimed her mouth again.

His kiss seemed to last forever, but other delights awaited and he moved his lips lower. Somehow Beth managed to stay sane as he kissed her everywhere and made her clothes vanish. His lips roved everywhere, sending her spiraling out of control. It was better than the childhood delight of being on a raft on the ocean. Never once did her body rest before beginning to crest again.

As he continued to love her now-glowing body, she grew bolder. She allowed herself to treasure him. She kissed him everywhere. Her lips tasted his cheeks, his eyebrows and his throat. She placed kisses on his chest. Her hands freed themselves, too, and she threaded them through the silken strands of his hair. She lowered her hands and felt his most intimate part, a part straining in the confines of his pants.

And she wanted it. She wanted him, all of him. He groaned and brought his lips to hers again.

"I want you," Beth said, and moments later, she had him. She detonated immediately as he filled her, stretching her tightness to accommodate his length.

It had been so long, but time didn't matter. At this moment, time seemed to pause, as if understanding the need of two lovers to suspend themselves in each other. The shades were drawn and she couldn't see him well in the darkened room, but that didn't matter, and as she became accustomed to him, her body's sensations began to change. She grew feverish with desire, and his strokes grew bolder and stronger, until they came together and lay exhausted in each other's arms.

"Okay?" he whispered.

"Okay," she replied, although she was sure she would never be okay again. By making love with Quinton she'd raised the bar. Never had it been this good, this wonderful. Never had she met a man who had made her feel more complete.

Unfortunately, he wasn't hers—not long-term, anyway.

Doubt began to creep in, and he slid away from her. But he didn't leave as Randy had often done. Instead, he rolled onto his back and pulled her into his arms. Her head on his chest, she heard his heart beating as it returned to normal.

"That was incredible," he said. He toyed with her

hair, running the strands through his fingers. "You are incredible, Beth."

And as he continued to hold her, she didn't know what to say.

Chapter Eight

"So, it was a whirlwind. That's so wonderful. And I love your ring! Babs said it's an heirloom."

"It is," Beth responded. She withdrew her left hand from the tenacious grasp of Mrs. Jonathan Simpson-Best.

"Well, you are a lucky woman, my dear. Quinton is quite a catch. We never thought he'd get married. And don't you worry about Susie over there," Mrs. Simpson-Best said.

Beth glanced over at Susannah Joelle Phelps. Susie Phelps was slim, whereas Beth had a mother's curves The girl had attended the couples' shower with her parents. Actually a catered party for sixty—Alan and Shelby's shower was at someone's mansion, someone Beth had met and couldn't remember if she'd tried.

"And think nothing of it if anyone says anything," the woman continued, "she's not half as heartbroken as she seems. She's just playing it for what it's worth. After all, she's only twenty-three. She's got lots of years left, and it's not as if there aren't other fish in the sea. She was just after Quinton because, well, he's Fred Searle's son."

"Thanks," Beth said. She smiled widely, and when Quinton saw her, she nodded her head to the left a bit without Mrs. Simpson-Best noticing. He understood, for within a moment he stood next to Beth.

"Hi, darling," he said. "I've been missing you. Having a good time?"

"Yes," she said, managing not to flush. Only a few hours ago she'd left Quinton's bed.

Mrs. Simpson-Best adjusted her glasses. "That is so sweet. Honey, if I were fifty years younger you wouldn't have a chance. Oh, Mildred—there you are. I've been looking for you. Have you seen Beth's heirloom ring?"

A spoon against a crystal goblet interrupted Mildred's inspection, and everyone in the room fell silent. "Time to open presents," someone Beth didn't know announced.

They all filed into the living room, where for the next thirty minutes they watched Alan and Shelby open a variety of gifts.

"Having fun?" Quinton asked.

"Can we leave soon?" Beth whispered.

"Want to get me back in bed already?" Quinton teased. He'd made love to her most of the afternoon, and then Beth had slipped back to her own room.

"No," she said. "I want to check on my daughter… and I don't belong here."

"You belong," Quinton said. "You're with me."

She rolled her eyes. "You know what I mean."

"Use the earlier reason and I promise that we'll sneak out," he teased back.

"Uh," Beth said, flushing at the memory of his lovemaking.

Babs suddenly appeared. "There are seats up right over by Alan and Shelby."

"Oh, you should sit there," Quinton said. Babs looked down her nose and fanned herself. "Never mind." He cupped Beth's elbow and led her to the designated spot. "You should have used the earlier excuse and we could have made a beeline for it," Quinton said.

"I'll remember that," Beth said. She and Quinton had a front-row spot to see all the gifts, ranging from crystal to pots and pans to a few pieces of sexy lingerie that no one would admit to giving.

The last gift, though, wasn't for them. Shelby reached for the rectangular box and brought it over to Beth. "This is for you and Quinton," she said.

Somehow Beth managed to say thank-you as she accepted the silver-foil-wrapped present.

"Open it," Shelby said eagerly.

Beth's fingers trembled as she carefully removed the bow. She slid her finger under the ribbon and removed it without breaking it.

"At your shower we'll make you a bow bouquet," Shelby said. Beneath the glittery paper was a beige nondescript box. Beth lifted the lid and found inside a scrapbook with the words *Our Wedding* emblazoned in silver foil on the cream-coloured cover.

"That's for you to start recording your memories," Shelby said. She faced the audience of friends and family. "Most of you may not know, but my brother is engaged to be married. When Alan and I became engaged, my friend Linda gave me a scrapbook. I'm glad I kept it. Now it's my turn to share the tradition. Welcome to the family, Beth."

People began clapping and Beth fought to keep the tears from flowing. She hadn't expected *this*. She turned to Quinton.

"Kiss," some nameless face shouted, and without further prompting, Quinton complied.

Dear Lord, Beth thought as his lips touched hers. She'd made love to the man all day, but the intensity of the emotion behind this kiss took her by surprise. Instinctively she brought her hand up to the side of his face and kissed him back.

Again everyone clapped, and Beth, returned to reality by the noise, drew back. Quinton's long lashes covered his gray eyes, and when he lifted them, the dark depths were unreadable. But she knew in her heart that the kiss was only a prelude.

"Thank you," she said. The show over, people began to disperse to once more eat and socialize.

"Let's make our exit," Quinton said, "and go check on Carly."

"Okay," Beth said. She repackaged the scrapbook, stood and followed Quinton.

Babs noticed them moving toward the door. "Leaving so soon?" she asked.

"Beth wants to check on Carly," Quinton replied. "I'm going to take her home."

"We have that party tomorrow," Babs said. "Will you be attending?"

"I think we're going to skip that and leave early instead," Quinton said. "It's supposed to snow and we can't afford to get stuck in St. Louis. Both of us have to work Monday."

"I…" Babs began to fan herself.

"It will be fine, Mom." Shelby had appeared and had overheard the entire conversation. "A ton of people will be there and no one will even notice. And they'll be back next Friday night in time for the rehearsal."

"Carly did so well," Babs agreed. "She loves her dress and can't wait to wear it."

"I know," Beth said. "She's also excited about getting her hair done with all the big girls." Quinton moved his hand suddenly to the small of Beth's back, and momentarily she lost what she'd meant to say. "If I haven't already said thank you, thank you. This means a great deal to Carly."

"It's no problem," Babs said. "I'm glad she's happy. Be safe going back. Deborah Mitchell was saying it's iced over a bit."

"We will," Quinton said. "See you later, Mom." He gave her a quick kiss on the cheek.

Then with gentle pressure of his hand on Beth's back, he guided her to where their coats were and within moments they were on their way.

No words were needed or spoken on the drive back,

and somehow this made the urgency between them more real. The baby-sitter had driven herself, and when they reached the house, while Quinton paid her, Beth went upstairs to check on Carly. The child had fallen asleep reading picture books, her trusted blanket tucked in next to hers.

"It always amazes me how peaceful children are when they sleep," Quinton said as he came to stand by Beth.

"So you can remember it in stormy times—like when they're screaming," Beth said. "When she was a baby, she had this total look of peace about her that only children can have. It was like being able to see God. So beautiful."

"Her mother is beautiful, too," Quinton said.

"Say that enough times and I might believe you," Beth said with a slight sigh.

"You should believe me now," Quinton said forcefully. His hands threaded up into her hair and he guided her from the nursery, then paused outside her bedroom. "Come with me. Come to my room for a while? You can bring the monitor if you want."

"This is like being kids," Beth said.

"I didn't make love in my parents' house when I was a kid," Quinton said. "Shelby was right. You're the only woman I've ever brought here."

But he'd brought her because they had made a deal, right? No, she would not let reality intrude. Not tonight. Beth pushed all negative thoughts out of her head.

"Oh" was all she said, but it was enough. She followed him, and when they arrived at his room, he reached around her and opened her door. She stepped through and then looked back. Quinton stood on the threshold, waiting. She reached her arms out and as their hands came together he stepped inside and shut the door.

It was when he kissed her that the urgency, the time constraint they were under, showed. Clothes flew, mouths kissed and bodies molded and joined, until a satiated Beth lay in Quinton's arms.

"Stay with me," he said.

"Your parents will be home soon. We played with danger enough this afternoon."

"That's not what I mean. Stay with me. Don't leave the way you'd planned. Stay until one of us gets bored, which I doubt. Stay until this fizzles, which I doubt. You've filled a hole in my life. Stay with me."

Panic began to overtake her. "I…"

"Just think about it," Quinton said. "I want you to stay."

"I'll think about it," she said, for it was easier than letting any chance of disappointment ruin the magical moment they'd shared.

She hated when she moved away, relinquishing the warmth of her spot. She leaned over and kissed his lips one last time. She dressed, and then she slipped out the door.

She needed to brush her teeth, do something, but when she arrived at her room, her limbs felt heavy and she simply lay down and went to sleep.

"SO HOW IS THAT HUNK of yours?" Nancy asked bright and early Monday morning while the two women began making Valentine's Day cookies of all shapes and sizes.

Under the guise of rolling out the cookie dough until it was the perfect thickness, Beth averted her head, the lie that Quinton wasn't her hunk failing to find a voice. "He's fine," she said, instead.

"Oh, my," Nancy said. "That's a big change from last week. Last week you were denying he was your hunk at all. You must have had a good weekend. How's his family?"

"Nice," Beth replied.

"They accepted you?"

"With open arms," Beth said. Despite the fact that that was exactly what they were supposed to have done, it still surprised Beth that they had done it so easily. After the basketball game, it was obvious Quinton's father adored her.

Of course, wasn't that the original plan? That way, when she dumped Quinton, they would rally around him and understand his loss and his desire to be alone with nothing but work to soothe him.

But she didn't know what the plan was anymore. She wore a diamond that didn't belong to her, lived in a glorious condo with a generous man and pretended to be his fiancée. He'd made love to her, and she to him. Many times over. And that had changed things. He'd asked her to stay with him.

That was impossible.

For lust was dangerous, but love was the most dangerous of all. And she was falling for Dr. Quinton Searle.

She was falling for a fairy tale, for a prince who, outside the mythical world they'd created, probably didn't exist.

She had known the whole truth last night, when they'd arrived back in Chicago.

"Can I call you Daddy?" Carly had asked Quinton after he'd finished reading her a story.

And when Quinton had told her she could call him whatever she wanted, Beth's heart had broken. For what might be best for her—a sexual affair with Quinton until their chemistry fizzled or until their playacting was done—was not what was best for her daughter. Carly needed stability. She would not understand what Beth knew—that they still had to leave.

Beth would never again marry for a reason other than love. And without marriage, she and Carly could not stay. And whereas she might be falling in love with Quinton, she knew he wasn't in love with her. She wasn't his type, even if she did fill a hole in his life.

He'd been lonely. She'd been wanton. But that wasn't a strong enough foundation for marriage.

She used cookie cutters to form heart-shaped dough that, when baked, she would frost red, pink, white and silver.

No, if Beth were single, she'd have no problem staying with Quinton for as long as he hungered for her.

She'd have no problem spending hours in his bed. But eventually it would end.

Good things in her life always did. She'd learned that early with her parents' marriage. The lesson had been further drilled into her head as she'd made the coveted high school cheerleading squad, only to have to transfer to a new city and a new school a month later because her mother got a new job. Even Randy had been a reminder that good things didn't last—their relationship had been fiery but life and pregnancy had made passion fade and problems begin.

Beth just had to remember her motto: Crashes Happen, But The Phoenix Always Rises. She came out stronger each time.

But this time she had a daughter to protect. A daughter who wouldn't understand what would have gone wrong when Quinton and she split up, which was as inevitable as the sun rising.

Or was it? The nagging doubt entered her head. Maybe she could make this work. Maybe she could…

No, she couldn't. She'd tried this once before, with Randy. The result had been disastrous. You couldn't make someone love you, be someone he wasn't.

In the end, as always, Beth had her daughter's future to secure. The last thing Carly should experience was the trauma Beth had suffered when her parents separated. At four, Carly was still young, resilient. The ties would be easier to sever now, rather than later after she'd become even more attached to Quinton.

Unless it was already too late.

But she couldn't stay just because she was afraid of removing Carly, either.

The catch-22 loomed large, and Beth finished the cookies. She'd taken the last half of the day off to go look at apartments.

If she found one, she'd tell Quinton tonight that Nancy had agreed to advance her the security deposit and first month's rent and let Beth work it off over a three-month period.

BY THAT AFTERNOON Beth had found an apartment, but as Quinton had gotten called to work ER duty, she didn't have a good moment to tell him. In fact, there didn't seem to be a good time the entire week. And telling him in bed was out of the question. That was one place Beth kept sacred, kept the fantasy and the reality separate.

The next time they had the chance to talk was on the flight to St. Louis. Rather than making the five-hour journey by car again, Quinton had surprised her and Carly Thursday evening with round-trip tickets. So on Friday they left Quinton's car in a long-term parking lot and boarded a ten a.m. flight. With arriving at the airport an hour early, checking in and going through security, the entire trip to St. Louis took two hours. Since Carly sat in the first class-seat between them and Quinton on the other side of the aisle, she never told him about her decision.

Quinton rented a car, and by one p.m. they were pulling into the driveway of the massive Ladue mansion of Babs and Fred Searle.

"Great, you're on time," Babs said as she greeted them at the door, a cordless phone next to her ear. "Quinton, go try on your tux. It's in your father's dressing room. The tailor is upstairs for any last-minute alterations." She turned her attention back to the phone call and quickly disappeared to take care of more prewedding agenda items.

"A tailor?" Beth asked.

"To make any last-minute adjustments," Quinton said. He grinned. "These aren't rental tuxes. They were custom made."

"Oh." She and Randy had been married in the courthouse. Randy hadn't even worn a suit.

Shelby appeared in the foyer. "Hi! Glad you made it. Did you see Mom?"

"She went that way, phone to her ear," Quinton said pointedly.

"She's more frazzled that I am," Shelby said. "She's driving the wedding coordinator nuts. So Carly, tell me, are you ready to be a flower girl?"

Carly giggled and nodded.

"That's good," Shelby said. She reached out her hand and Carly took it. "You haven't met Marni, the housekeeper. She's in the kitchen, and I bet you're hungry."

"I am hungry," Carly said, even though she'd snacked on crackers and peanuts the entire flight. She began to follow Aunt Shelby.

"Let's go get some food. I'm hungry, too." Shelby stopped for a moment and leaned back so she could see

Quinton. "By the way, big brother, Mom's serious about that tux. Go make sure it fits. And we leave for the church in an hour and a half. The rehearsal starts at five."

"I better do as asked," Quinton said. "You might want to freshen up and change into whatever you're wearing."

Beth glanced down at her chinos and sweater. She'd brought the gray dress for the wedding and a pantsuit for tonight. She hoped it would be fashionable enough, but somehow doubted it. "Okay," she said. "I guess I could rest up a little."

"Good idea." He gave her a quick kiss on the forehead. "I'll take the stuff up and go meet with the tailor."

Beth didn't see Quinton again until the rehearsal, and then between the pastor and the wedding coordinator, all Beth did was sit in a pew and watch the proceedings. She did sit with Quinton at the rehearsal dinner, and he snuck into her room and made love to her that night.

The next morning Beth slept in, and when she woke up she discovered that Carly had been whisked off to the beauty parlor for her big-girl makeover. Beth wandered around the house, until finally she dressed in the plain gray dress and put on the simple fake-pearl earrings she'd worn on her and Quinton's first date. How long ago that seemed. And after tonight, it would be all over. She'd signed the lease; she moved in next week. She had to tell Quinton.

Today would be bittersweet.

Quinton knocked on her door at a little after three. "Ready?" His eyes assessed her and he grinned. "You are beautiful," he said.

"I don't know about that, but I'm ready," Beth said. She smiled at the man her heart had grown to love. Standing there in his tux, he was the most handsome, wonderful man she'd ever seen. Carly had pegged him right. He was a prince.

They rode together to the church, where once again they were separated as Quinton went off to do his duties as a groomsman.

Beth stood, abandoned in the narthex, waiting for her time to be seated.

"Hello," a voice said. "Beth, right?"

Beth turned. The thirty-something man standing beside her seemed familiar, but she'd met so many people lately, she couldn't place him.

"You don't remember me, do you?"

Beth shook her head. "No."

"I'm Dr. Winters, Jud Winters. I was Randy's neurologist. You and I only met a few times."

"Oh," Beth said. "Of course."

"I'm sorry about what happened," he said. "Randy was a good man. And this may sound awkward, but I hope you'll believe that I'm sincere when I offer you congratulations. I can't tell you how delighted I am that you're marrying Quinton. We went to med school together. He's a great man, Beth. The best. I hope you'll be happy. Randy told me what you were going through. You deserve to be happy."

"Thank you," Beth said. The ushers were seating people, and she had one of them take her in and lead her to the second pew on the bride's side.

She sat there for about ten minutes, simply staring at the interior of the church. It was splendid. White candles lit the way down the aisle. The building itself was A-frame in design—the ceiling cherrywood that formed a triangle against a back wall of sand-colored stones held together by mortar.

A large cherrywood cross was hung suspended from the ceiling above the altar, which was breathtaking, too. A huge, curved-wood wall divided the altar from the back wall of the church. Organ pipes were visible on each side of the twenty-foot-high, thirty-foot-wide wall, and the top of the wall was covered with green garland and twenty red-foil pots of white roses. A modern bronze diorama covered the front of the wall. The only other flowers were rows of red roses that matched the woven red-, blue-, green- and gold-tapestry that covered the altar.

Then the wedding began. The groomsmen filed in, and Beth's heart leaped as she saw Quinton. He was so gorgeous in his custom tux. He gave her a warm smile as he went by, a smile that curled her toes and promised other things for later.

The organ music changed again, and the bridesmaids filed in. Beth swiveled around as the first flower girl came down the aisle. She dropped red petals on the white runner. Beth held her breath. Carly was next.

And then her lovely daughter appeared. Tears came

to Beth's eyes. Carly wore a ring of flowers in her hair and a long-sleeved, floor-length dress. She took a step.

And faltered.

Beth blinked a few tears away. Her mother's instinct never failed. Something was wrong. Terribly wrong.

Chapter Nine

Whereas Carly had skipped down the aisle last night during rehearsal, today she stood frozen as a church full of people stared at her.

"Go," the wedding coordinator was urging her.

In the pew in front of her, Beth heard Babs mutter, "Oh, no."

Beth was first and foremost a mother. Her child needed her. She was on her feet in seconds. She stepped out onto the white runner, her gray shoes a marked contrast.

She knew all eyes were now on her, but Beth never wavered. She strode down the aisle, her walk sure. She was Carly's mother, and no matter what, she wouldn't let her daughter down.

"Go," the wedding coordinator commanded again, but still Carly refused to budge.

Beth reached her daughter and extended her hand. "Hi, honey. Shall we walk down the aisle together?"

Carly nodded and blinked back the tears that were brimming but not yet flowing. She held out her free hand. "Can you do that?" Carly asked.

Beth clasped her daughter's hand in hers. "I'm your mommy, honey. I can do whatever you need me to do. I love you."

"I love you, too," Carly said. "All these people are staring at me. I was afraid."

"I know," Beth said. She turned around. The crowd gathered in the church simply stared and the organist kept repeating the same refrain, but Beth didn't care. She was a mother, and that always came first.

"You can do it, Carly. I'm with you."

Hand in hand, she and Carly took their first steps down the aisle together.

QUINTON RELEASED the breath he'd been holding. His chest, though, didn't stop constricting.

He'd never seen a more magnificent sight.

There they were, hand in hand, walking down the aisle. Occasionally Beth would stop, and Carly would release her mother's hand and reach into the white basket. She would toss white rose petals onto the white runner, slide the basket over her arm again and then take Beth's hand. With stops about every seven feet, it took them a few minutes to reach the front of the church.

As Beth approached, a wave of longing swept over him. He had the sudden image of himself as a groom, Beth as the bride.

The vision should have scared him, but oddly, it didn't.

He gave her a warm, encouraging smile as she and

Carly sat down in the second pew. Then everyone stood and the bride came down the aisle. As he watched his sister get married, he contemplated life as Beth's husband.

He liked her. He enjoyed making love to her. He adored her daughter. He and Beth never fought, and with his salary and trust fund, they would never lack for anything. She loved Chicago, as he did. She fit in his apartment as though she'd moved in with him from the beginning. He enjoyed her company. Weren't all those things the foundation of a good marriage?

Of course, he hadn't given any thought to love. Was he in love with her? Quinton watched his sister promise to love and cherish Alan until "death do us part."

Death had parted Randy and Beth, and it hadn't been a marriage full of love and happiness. Some of his partners were on to wife number two because they'd fallen in and out of love. No, it was best if that fairytale type of love wasn't factored into marriage. Marriage was a friendship, a bonding. Passion died. He didn't want that. Did he love Beth? Of course he did, as one loves something precious. Marriage to Beth would cement their burgeoning friendship and also, give Carly a father.

He decided to ask Beth later tonight. He grinned to himself—thanks to his mother, Beth already had the ring.

"WASN'T IT a gorgeous ceremony?" Babs enthused two hours later at the reception. She sat just to Beth's left at the round table for eight. Carly sat to Beth's left. They were minus Quinton, for he sat with the wedding party at the head table.

"Beautiful," Beth agreed. "The exchanging of the rings was especially touching."

Carly divided her roll and Beth reached over to butter it for her. The waiter began to set plates of salad onto the white-linen covered table.

"So, have you given any thought to when and where you want to have your ceremony?" Babs asked.

"Not really," Beth said.

"Do you have family in Chicago?"

Beth shook her head. She'd used a curling iron on the ends, and one of the curls bounced against her cheek. "My parents are divorced and live on opposite coasts. They tried to get as far away from each other as possible."

"Oh," Babs said. "So I take it they won't be involved in the wedding preparations?"

A polite way of asking if they planned on offering any financial assistance. "I doubt it," Beth said. "I was married once before. But I'm hoping that they'll at least show up."

Babs appeared horrified. "I would hope so." The lines on her face smoothed out, and she leaned over and patted Beth's hand. "Don't worry, you've got a new family now. We do everything together."

Beth was saved from replying because Carly accidentally dropped her spoon, and Beth retrieved it from the floor. When she straightened, she set the spoon aside and reached for her fork to begin eating.

The salad was as tasty as it looked, and the dinner was chicken breast covered with a smooth, golden sauce. But chicken wasn't the only thing on the plate. There was also a perfectly cooked filet mignon, some mashed potatoes pressed into flower shapes and thin green beans tossed with almonds. Beth sampled every one of the delicious foods, but she left most of each on her plate; her appetite vanished as Babs went on and on about Beth and Quinton's wedding.

Beth was sure Babs had the entire event planned by the time Alan and Shelby cut the cake, Babs hovering nearby.

"So, did you survive sitting by my mother?" Quinton said as he came up to her and Carly after the main course. The caterer had given Carly one of the first pieces of cake. "Tell me it wasn't bad."

"It wasn't bad," Beth said. She had to admit that she liked Quinton's mother. Babs was a bit spoiled and definitely used her heart condition to her advantage, but other than that, she was well-meaning. Beth had also been impressed that Babs hadn't uttered one word about Carly's failure to be the perfect flower girl.

"So what did she talk to you about?" Quinton asked as he lowered himself into Bab's chair.

"Our wedding," Beth said.

"That's what I figured," Quinton said. "I want to discuss that with you later."

"That would be a good idea," Beth said. "This whole thing is out of control. At least your mother didn't force me to be in the family pictures after I objected—"

"Quinton! You remember Mrs. Simmons, don't you? She lived two doors down from us until she retired to Florida?"

Quinton gave Beth a wry smile before he rose and greeted Babs and the woman at her heels.

"So is it good?" Beth asked her daughter.

Carly had cake crumbs all over her lips. "Mmm-hmm."

"Well, since I want to be a pastry chef, I guess I should sample this. I don't think one bite will hurt." Alan and Shelby had chosen a multi-layer white cake with white cream icing. It melted in Beth's mouth. "Oh, this is good."

"Mmm-hmm," Carly said again. Her plate held only a few white crumbs. "Can I have more?"

"*May* I have more?" Beth corrected.

"May I?" Carly gave Beth her cute-puppy pout.

Beth sighed. The last thing Carly needed was more cake, but today was a special day.

"You can have some of mine," Beth said. She used the fork to separate another morsel, and then moved the fork to Carly's lips.

"You're feeding me like I'm a baby," Carly said. "I'm not a baby."

"I know. You're my big girl," Beth said. Carly slurped the cake from the fork. "You've gotten so big. You're already too big to feed. You've got to stop growing. "

"I can't," Carly said with a giggle.

"What are my girls laughing about?" Quinton said, approaching their table.

"I'm growing," Carly said. "I'm getting to be too big for Mommy."

"I see," Quinton said. His gray eyes twinkled. The married couple were having their first dance, but he didn't seem to notice or care. "So what are you going to do?"

Her expression thoughtful, Carly accepted another forkful of cake before answering. "I think I'll grow up. You're growing, too, aren't you, Mommy?"

Beth managed a smile. Quinton detected the sadness behind it, although Carly didn't. "Mommy's growing old, honey."

"You aren't old," Carly said.

"I am old," Beth said. "And someday you'll have a wedding and move away and have your own family."

"I'll never leave you," Carly promised. "I'll always live with you." She paused as if remembering something. "Sarah's mom got lonely because Sarah had grown up so much, so she went and got a new baby. You could get a new baby."

"Out of the mouths of babes," Beth murmured.

"Who's Sarah?" Quinton asked.

"She moved into one of the condos in our old building. She's a year older than Carly. She has just about every toy known to man," Beth said.

"She also has candy. That's what I was searching for when I went into Mommy's purse," Carly said. "She was showing me all her candy that day. Mommy *never* buys me candy."

"Ah, the truth finally comes out," Quinton said.

Babs appeared, putting a hand to the pearls at her throat. "The family dance is up next. You and Beth are going to dance, aren't you?"

"I want to dance," Carly said.

"We'll *all* dance," Quinton decided.

Somehow they succeeded in doing just that for about three songs. Quinton either put Carly on his shoulders, or she stood on his feet. Once, she rested on his hip and he had one arm around her and the other around Beth. Later, Beth opted out to use the ladies' room. As she left, Babs met her in the hall.

"Ah, here you are. Everyone is commenting on how sweet the three of you were out there."

"Thanks," Beth said. Babs gestured to a sofa, and Beth sat on it. "My feet got tired. I should be used to standing since I'm on my feet most of the day when I'm baking."

"That reminds me, we haven't really gotten a chance to talk about your work situation. Will you still be working after you and Quinton are married? You don't have to, you know. He makes plenty of money."

"I still plan on continuing to work," Beth said. "I enjoy baking. Plus, Carly will be in kindergarten next fall. There's no reason for me to just lounge around an empty apartment."

"You mean house. You and Quinton are planning on buying a house, aren't you?"

Where was this going? Beth's forehead creased as she gazed at Quinton's mother. "I don't believe so. Quinton loves his view of Lake Michigan, and I have to admit, I'm pretty partial to the water myself."

"But that's only temporary. Quinton has told you he's returning home, hasn't he? Back to St. Louis? He's to take over his father's pediatric practice. Fred is ready to start cutting back."

Here it was, the opportunity to do the job she'd agreed to do. Beth had saved Carly earlier that day; now she must save Quinton. As for saving herself...

"We really don't want to leave Chicago," Beth said slowly.

Babs's eyes narrowed in speculation. "Why not? You have no family there. Who will help you when you two decide to have more children? St. Louis is a much better place to raise children. Fred and I have three acres only ten minutes from the West County hospitals and twenty from those in the city's Central West End. It's an ideal location. Chicago is so big, so spread out. And the schools..." Babs shuddered. "I've heard some awful things. You certainly can't educate your child there, especially not in public school."

"We haven't discussed it," Beth said. "And I attend pastry college there, you know. It's extremely important to me that I finish my program. That will take at least a few more quarters."

"A wife's place is with her husband, and Quinton's place is in St. Louis," Babs insisted.

"Babs." Beth's tone conveyed a warning.

Babs heard it, for she began to fan herself with her hand. "Really, this just won't do," she said. "He must come home. He's been gone long enough. He has responsibilities to his family and—"

"Babs." Beth's voice was firm, and Babs looked at her in surprise. "Quinton has told me all about your heart condition. I don't intend any disrespect, but our decision to stay in Chicago is not going to kill you. My husband died of cancer. I watched him waste away before my eyes. You have years left. Don't alienate your son by demanding he do something he doesn't want to do."

Babs wore a shocked expression. "I didn't mean—"

Beth cut her off. "Babs, I know *you* mean well. But Quinton is a grown man. It's his life to live. You have to let him live it."

"I just want what's best for him. I'm his mother and—"

"Of course you want what's best. No one is debating that. You're an excellent mother, Babs. All one needs for proof is seeing how wonderfully your children turned out. But you have to stop pressuring Quinton. He is quite capable of running his life, and he and I will make our own decisions. You really need to let us do that."

Babs sat there in stunned silence for a moment. Beth simply waited, and for a good few minutes neither woman said anything.

When Babs finally spoke, Beth expected her to be offended, to even snap back. Instead, she seemed resigned.

"You're probably right," Babs said. "I have been nagging him for a while. I just love him and want him to be closer to me. That old house gets lonely. He's been gone eighteen years. I miss my son."

"I understand," Beth said. "I'm petrified of the day Carly will leave and go to college. She's been all I've had for so long. But I have to let her go. That's what I've been raising her for, no matter how hard it'll be to let her go."

"I agree," Babs said. She blinked away a tear. "You're a good woman, Beth. I had my doubts when I first met you, but I can see that you're all heart—and after what you did in the church today, a true and loving mother."

A movement caught Babs's attention. "We'll continue this later, dear. They're going to toss the bouquet." She stood. "Come watch with me."

Beth shook her head. "Go ahead. I feel a sudden urge to hug my daughter."

Babs smiled and nodded her approval. "You do that," she said.

"Mommy!" Carly ran up at that moment. "I've got to go potty."

"Okay," Beth said. She walked her daughter the few feet to the restroom. "Did you run out here alone?"

"Oh, no," Carly said as the door shut behind them. "Quinton came, too."

"Okay," Beth said. "As long as you weren't running around by yourself."

QUINTON WATCHED as the three women in his life headed in different directions: his mother back into the banquet hall, Beth and Carly through the ladies' room door.

"Hanging out?" his father asked.

Quinton gestured toward the restroom. "Waiting," he said.

"Ah," his father replied. "You'll do that a lot."

"No kidding," Quinton said.

"I was looking for your mother," Fred said. "Have you seen her?"

"She just went back inside," Quinton replied. "Bouquet toss or something."

His father smiled, nodded and disappeared back into the banquet room.

Quinton kept his gaze on the rest-room door. As soon as Beth reappeared, he would take her home. A sense of urgency filled him. He'd heard every word of her conversation with his mother.

Once again Beth had left him nothing short of amazed. In two weeks, she had done the impossible. No one put Babs Searle in her place, but Beth had gently done so—and won Babs's approval, as well.

Beth and Carly were laughing when they emerged from the rest room. He peeled himself away from the wall he was leaning against. "What's so funny?"

"Nothing," Beth said with a warning shake of her head. But Carly wasn't to be silenced.

"My skirt got stuck in my tights," Carly told him. "Mommy had to pull it out. You could see my underwear when I walked."

"Carly! You're not supposed to tell," Beth admonished her. "It was our secret."

Quinton burst into laughter. As a doctor, he'd heard many funny childhood tales, but this coming from

Carly made it more precious. Finally, he said, "Are my girls ready to go home?"

"No," Carly replied. "I want more cake. I'm not tired. I want to dance."

"I think we're ready to go home," Beth said with a nod that meant no further arguments. "It's past your bedtime by about three hours."

Carly pouted but didn't complain.

"I'll get our coats," Quinton said.

Soon he and Beth would have a chance to talk.

QUINTON STOOD in the bedroom doorway while Beth tucked a very sleepy Carly into bed. When Carly pulled her blanket close, something sharp tugged on Quinton's heartstrings.

Beth leaned over and kissed her daughter. "I love you, honey," she said. "You did a wonderful job as a flower girl today."

"I love you, too, Mommy." Carly rolled over and shut her eyes. Beth moved toward the door. Suddenly, Carly rolled back over and her blue eyes were wide-open.

"What is it?" Beth asked.

Carly sat up a little and gazed at the doorway, at the man standing there. "Quinton, will you kiss me good-night?"

He'd never been asked that before. At her words, he could hear his heart pounding in his ears. Oh, but this little blond beauty had a hold on him. He went to Carly's bedside, bent down to kiss her forehead. She wrapped her arms around his neck and her slim body pressed into his for a big hug.

"I love you," she said. Then she smiled and snuggled into her covers.

His "Good night, sleep tight" caught in his throat. So he simply kissed her forehead again. "Good night, honey," he whispered as he straightened. She was already almost asleep.

He returned to the doorway, where Beth stood, a stricken expression on her beautiful face. He knew she was thinking about Carly's words and the impact of those words. He knew Beth had a profound fear of their implications. But in a few minutes, everything would be okay. They would be a family, and he would be Carly's father. He smiled and reached for Beth's hand.

"Let's go talk," he said.

It was time to make this pretend engagement real.

Chapter Ten

Quinton wanted to "talk." Turmoil unlike any she'd experienced in her life—and that was saying a lot, since Beth had experienced plenty—spiraled through her, causing her heart to beat erratically.

When she took Quinton's hand, reassurance and tenderness emanated from it, but even that didn't relax Beth. If anything, the vise on her heart and soul tightened, until she felt her insides knot with pain.

Her daughter had told this man she loved him.

Quinton Frederick Searle IV was a very loved man if Carly loved him. A child's love was always unconditional, the purest love in the world.

Unfortunately, the relationship between Beth and Quinton *was* conditional, with more layers than there had been to Shelby's wedding cake.

Quinton led Beth into his bedroom and closed the door behind him. He turned Beth to face him, and at that moment, Beth knew she'd grown too dependent on this man. Being with him made her happy. Being with him made her daughter happy. But their relationship, as she'd told herself oh, so many times, was like a fairy-tale. Some people were destined to be happy, others weren't. It was the law of opposites or something like that.

She was one of those not destined for happiness. The joy in her life was always fleeting. To pretend or dream otherwise was foolish.

Dreams were dangerous.

Dreaming caused people to be dissatisfied with what they had. Dreaming got people hurt.

No, her relationship with Quinton was based on a condition, wasn't real. And whatever the attraction between them, it came from a chemistry—whose merit vanished when scrutinized in the light of day.

Desperation filled Beth. She needed this one last night, before morning revealed the truth of her life again.

Before Quinton's parents came home, she wanted to create a memory that would last her forever when the fairy tale disappeared.

"Make love to me," she said.

"I—" Quinton began.

Beth cut him off with a passionate kiss.

She was the leader this time, and despite his initial surprise, Quinton gave no further protest. He sipped from her lips as if they contained the sweetest nectar. But Beth wanted more. Wanted all of him.

She explored his mouth. She wasn't subtle or coy. She demanded and took, and Quinton finally groaned and lifted his head.

"I want you, too," he said.

Beth walked to the bed where they'd first come together. She turned around. The gray dress didn't have buttons. It had to be lifted over her head. She simply raised her arms in the air, and within seconds Quinton had pulled the garment off.

He brought his mouth down on hers and joined her in the magical journey of two souls who need each other. Beth reveled in the sensations as he kissed her neck, flicking his tongue into the hollow of her throat. He lowered his mouth and kissed her breasts through her lace bra. She quivered. He edged away the scrap of fabric, and tasted, his tongue wet on her skin. Beth closed her eyes in bliss.

Quinton's fingers moved everywhere—his intent to heighten her pleasure, and she touched him everywhere in response. But suddenly the urgency inside her crested and then ebbed. Her passion didn't die, though, it changed. Tonight wasn't only about taking; but it was also about giving.

At that moment Beth realized the truth. Quinton Searle would be her last lover. No one would top him, Beth knew that in the marrow of her bones.

But the thought disappeared into the recesses of her mind as Quinton sheathed himself and entered her with one solid thrust. He'd left the bedside light on, and his gray eyes didn't leave her face as he drove himself in and out.

She couldn't stand it, yet she could—the emotions and the passion flowing through her, lifting her beyond reason. She closed her own eyes as the world she knew spun away. There was only here and now, there was only her and Quinton. She ached, she shuddered; her body quivered and quaked as both of them entered that magical place where time doesn't just stop—it doesn't exist at all.

He lowered himself onto her and she clung to him, unwilling to let him go, unwilling to part their touching bodies. But eventually reality crept in, and the present returned.

"Hey," Quinton said as he finally rolled away from her. "Give me a minute and I'll be back. I want to hold you and talk."

"Okay," she said.

Beth waited until Quinton disappeared into the en suite. He quickly returned, slid into bed and gathered her into his arms.

"Marry me," he said without preamble.

"What?" Had she heard him correctly? Had he gone crazy? Beth struggled to get out of his arms, but Quinton held her firm.

"Marry me," he repeated.

She stared at him. She *had* heard him correctly. "You want me to…marry you?"

Quinton frowned as if this wasn't quite the reaction or answer he'd expected. "Yes. I do."

He leaned on one elbow and paused, as though suddenly aware of his mistake. "I know this isn't the most romantic place or the proper way to ask you something this important. I should have wine, candles and be down on one knee. But not having those doesn't change the fact that I want you to marry me."

"Why?" As the word slipped out, Beth realized how insensitive she sounded. "Sorry. I didn't mean to be rude. This is just…very surprising, that's all."

"No problem," Quinton said, but he didn't look convinced. In fact, he looked as though he didn't know what to do next. He continued to gaze down at her. "I want to marry you, Beth. Will you marry me?"

"Do you love me?" She winced. Who had taken control of her tongue? When he didn't reply right away, she slid away from him and sat up. "You don't love me, do you?"

Again, he appeared utterly lost and confused. "I care for you. You mean a great deal to me," he said.

"But…" Beth prompted. From the tone of his voice she knew there had to be more.

"I'm not sure I'm in love with you," he admitted. He sat up, the white sheet falling to his waist.

She nodded. "I could tell."

His lips parted slightly and his broad shoulders slumped. "How?"

Because Randy had felt the same way. It was obvious to her. "I just can. Call it feminine intuition."

"I want to marry you, Beth. Let's make this relationship, us, real. I adore your daughter. I adore you. I enjoy living with you and I enjoy making love to you. You've become a very important person in my life and I want you to stay. I want us to be permanent."

If only he were in love with her. Then, perhaps, she

could take a chance and let her feelings show, admit she was in love with him. But what he felt wasn't love. He cared for her. Well, she wouldn't settle for companionship again. She wanted everything, and would wait for it, even if that meant being alone for a long time.

"It isn't enough," she said. "I don't want to play house, Quinton."

From his expression, she realized he didn't understand.

"Beth, we have a firm friendship. We have great sex and an ability to get along that will last us when passion fizzles. A lot of marriages are built on less."

"I know," she stated flatly. "I was in one."

"I'm sorry." He lowered his gaze and seemed to study the pattern on the comforter. "I keep forgetting that you have a bad history. I guess I sort of feel that you and Carly have always been mine."

Oh, how she'd love to be his! But not without his being in love with her. She couldn't, wouldn't, settle for less.

"We have everything," he continued. "I do love you in the sense that you are important to me. Carly is important to me. I want to marry you, Beth. I've never said those words to anyone else."

"No." Beth's tone was gentle in its bittersweetness. "We don't have the kind of love that aches and burns. We don't have what your sister and Alan have. We have a companionship, and yes, a piece of a paper would legitimize that and make it okay in the eyes of the world. But I don't want a marriage because it's convenient and comfortable. I can't marry without real love," she said. "Like I said, I did that once, Quinton. I can never do it again. I settled for security and got heartache."

He held out his hands, but she didn't take them. "I won't hurt you. Surely you know me enough to be certain of that."

How she hated seeing the pain on his face. "I do, but I made myself a promise not to settle again. I don't want just a roof over my head, I don't want just security and a father for my child. And you should, too. You've known me only a few weeks. Really, you're only feeling this way because you've been stressed out over your family issues. Well, you've dealt with them. Tonight you were under the influence of wedding magic—when you see someone happy and you latch on to the first thing that looks right, even if it's not, because you want to be happy, too. I'm like a kitten you found—you'd like to keep me. But I already have a home."

"You were tossed out of your home," he noted.

"I was using an analogy. My point is that we got into this relationship for all the wrong reasons. Then we discovered that we have great chemistry. But chemistry and compatibility don't equal happily-ever-after."

He still looked shell-shocked. "You don't think we'd be happy?"

"No." Beth shook her head, as if shaking away the doubt she might have that he was right. She had to stand firm. Her blond hair fell into her eyes, hiding her hot tears. "We come from two different worlds. One of us would always feel less than the other. It would breed resentment."

"I care about you and your daughter," he reiterated. "I want you in my life."

"And I care about you. But I care about my daughter more. She can't lose anyone else."

"I'm not going anywhere. I'll never leave. I'll never cheat on you. We'll be happy."

Beth shook her head again. "We could discuss this forever, but I doubt I could ever make you understand. I can't marry you, Quinton. Just respect my decision whether you agree with it or not. You'll have to believe that I know what is best for my daughter and me. And marrying you isn't it."

"And if I were in love with you?" he pressed. "With that undying love you claim to want?"

"Don't even go there when you aren't," Beth replied. She touched the side of his face. His skin felt warm. "I found an apartment last week and I rented it. Nancy, my boss, lent me the money. I'm moving out when we get back."

"You're moving out," he repeated dully. He lifted her hand away and she dropped it into her lap.

"Yes." She couldn't meet his eyes.

"You borrowed the money—"

Bitter accusation hung in the air and Beth's heart lurched.

"Do you hate me that much, Beth? Did you think I

wouldn't give it to you if you asked? I just want you to be happy."

She tried again for common footing, to somehow make him see. "Did you ever read *To Kill a Mockingbird* by Harper Lee?"

"What does that have to do with anything?" Quinton's frustration made his tone short.

"In the book, Walter Cunningam, the little boy, is so poor that he doesn't have any lunch. The new first-grade teacher tells him to go eat downtown and offers him a quarter so he can buy food. He refuses and she doesn't understand."

Quinton's voice remained toneless. "And this relates to us how?"

"The Cunninghams take nothing that they know they can't repay. When Atticus Finch, the hero in the book, had to do some legal work for them, they pay him back here and there with potatoes and such until the debt is paid. I'm like the Cunninghams. I can't repay you, so I'm not going to take anything from you. Nancy, I can repay. I work for her. I've already been in your world long enough. It's time to go."

"*To Kill a Mockingbird* is about Southern race relations," Quinton said. "The story doesn't apply here. Not to us."

"It's a portrait of how the world works. Parts of the book still apply. I know where I belong, and it's not with you. Not without real love. I can't trespass in your world any longer. I have to go back to mine."

"I see," he said, although she knew he still didn't.

How would he? He was from privilege. "I guess this is it. We won't still see each other?"

Beth knew she was about to twist the knife in his heart. But if the pain was horrible now, how much worse would it be down the road if she stayed? "I think it would be best if we didn't have any contact with each other. I've experienced the finer things. Now that I know the difference, syrup won't cover the bad taste as well as it did before. And I don't want Carly exposed to any more than she already has been. If we don't go now—"

"Well." He sat there, his uneven breathing evident in the erratic rise and fall of his bare chest. "I certainly didn't expect this response when I said we had to talk. I had no idea you and I were on such completely different pages."

"I'm sorry," Beth said.

"Yeah. I bet you are."

He gave a hollow laugh that filled Beth's heart with even more guilt. "You're probably correct. It is probably best. Suddenly I don't really feel I know you at all."

Lord give her strength to endure the heartbreak. She wanted to cry, but instead she sank her top teeth into her lower lip. *This, too, shall pass,* she told herself. *This, too, shall pass. He'll be better off. I'll be better off. I can't take the risk. Not with Carly. I have to protect my daughter.*

This didn't stop Beth from feeling as though part of her was being ripped out when Quinton stood, dressed and left the room. Beth sat there, the light now harsh. Her face looked haggard in the mirror's reflection. She got up, dressed and quickly went to her own room.

She wasn't better the next morning, either, and guilt consumed her anew as Babs hugged her, wished her a Happy Valentine's Day in advance and told Beth that she looked forward to seeing her at Easter. Babs then hugged Carly, and Beth hated seeing the anticipation on her daughter's face. A Searle Easter would be candy and chocolate rabbits galore. With little money to spare, their own celebration would be very simple.

Did pride go before a fall?

And could falling hurt any more?

She and Quinton barely talked on the flight home Sunday, and when he did speak to her his words were clipped. He said nothing to Carly, but back in the apartment he clung to her for a long moment when she told him she loved him and gave him the paper heart she'd made on the plane. Then he told Beth he was going for a drive, and he disappeared.

They didn't see him again, and Beth felt like a thief in the night as she packed to move out while he was at work Monday, which of all days happened to be Valentine's Day. She placed the heirloom ring on his dresser. She tried to write a goodbye note, but the appropriate words never came, and Beth tore up the paper and put the scraps in the trash compactor.

She hated herself for hurting him. Hated herself for doing it on the holiday of romantic togetherness. Maybe she should have sacrificed. She'd sacrificed all her life, what was one more time? Her child would be so much happier to stay with Quinton…

No. Beth shut the door to his house decidedly behind her, her key left on the table by the front door.

Chapter Eleven

Their new apartment was near the L and the walls shook every time the trains rumbled by. The place wasn't much, just the upstairs shotgun flat of a two-family building, with a postage-stamp-size yard that would become a mud puddle after a summer downpour. She moved her stuff out of storage bit by bit, and within two weeks, the shabby apartment looked somewhat like home.

"In the summer you can play outside," Beth said, raising her voice as the train thundered by.

Carly tossed down her fork. Ever since Beth had picked her up at Ida's house Monday, the day after they'd returned, she'd been surly. "I hate it here," she said. "I want to go back to Quinton's! Why did we have to move?"

"It was time," Beth said. "Quinton and Mommy decided not to get married."

"I wanted to be a flower girl again," Carly said. Her lower lip stuck out. "I liked living with Quinton. I wanted him to be my daddy!"

"We have our own place now," Beth said. "It's just us girls. I love you, darling. You'll understand someday."

"I hate you," Carly said. She banged the table. "You didn't even get me a valentine." She burst into tears. "You should see all the valentines Sarah got! You should see her candy! We don't have any!"

"Candy's bad for your teeth and Valentine's was last week. It's over."

Beth closed her eyes for a moment. How could a four-year-old hope to understand? Perhaps someday…

Beth got up and went over to her daughter. She pulled Carly into her arms and she and Carly sat on the threadbare cloth that passed for an area rug. "I know it hurts, darling. I know. I'm sorry you're hurting."

"Why, Mommy? Why? Why did you leave him? Why isn't he my daddy?"

Because I love you too much, Beth thought. *Because I couldn't risk losing you later, when we broke up and you perhaps wanted him, instead of me.* Tears spilled down Beth's cheeks. Maybe she was an unfit mother after all. Maybe she was selfish, just as Babs Searle had been. Perhaps she'd been guilty of the same things.

"Mommy, don't cry," Carly pleaded. "I'm sorry, Mommy. I love you. Don't cry, Mommy. Please don't cry."

Beth heard the fear in Carly's trembling voice and sniffed back tears. "Mommy's okay, Carly. Mommy loves you so much."

"And I don't hate you. I was being mean."

"I know, sweetie. I know." She hugged her daughter. "And it'll all be okay. Easter'll soon be here, and I have a feeling the Easter bunny will bring you a basket."

That made Carly brighten.

Just then, a knock sounded at the door and Beth frowned. Carly jumped off her lap and ran to the door, the Quinton crisis forgotten with the newness of the moment. "Someone's here. We never get visitors. Who is it, Mommy? Come see."

Beth wiped her tears with the bottom of her sweater. She had no idea who it could be. Ida had gone to visit her relatives in Florida. Surely Quinton wouldn't…

She opened the front door.

"Jena!" Carly flew into Jena's arms.

"Hi, squirt," Jena said. "How are you?"

Carly wrinkled her nose and kept her arms tight around Jena's neck. "I've been okay."

"Well, I haven't. I've missed you," Jena said. She set Carly down on the floor. "And seeing that it was Valentine's Day recently, Cupid left something at my apartment for you, since he knew the Easter bunny wasn't coming for a bit."

Carly's blue eyes widened as Jena dug into her oversize black purse. "Really? Cupid went to your house? Does he look like he did in *The Santa Claus 2*?"

"Just like that," Jena said. She handed Carly a long thin box that looked suspiciously as if it contained a Barbie doll.

Carly clutched the wrapped present to her chest. "Can I open it?"

Beth began to correct her daughter's grammar, but Jena had already shot Beth a warning glance. Beth remained silent.

"Of course you can," Jena said. She stepped into the apartment and closed the door behind her. "Hello, Beth," Jena said in a carefully neutral tone that made it clear she knew exactly what had transpired between Beth and Quinton.

"Jena," Beth said.

Carly shredded the red-and-white wrapping paper, in her excitement dropping the scraps on the floor. Carly held up the box. "Look, Mommy! It's Barbie! She has a dog, too!"

"That's great, honey," Beth said. She gestured to what served as a living room. "Please sit down."

"Thank you," Jena said. She took off her heavy winter coat and put it on a chair before settling into an armchair near the sofa.

"Would you like anything to drink?" Beth asked. "Carly and I made pumpkin bread today. We just finished dinner and were going to have some for dessert."

"It's good," Carly announced. "I helped. Mommy let me add in the sugar and the spices because I'm a girl."

"That's wonderful, Carly. I would love some of the dessert you made," Jena replied.

Beth served the pumpkin bread, which they all enjoyed. Twenty minutes later, when Carly skipped off to her room to gather something for Jena to see, Jena got right to the point with Beth.

"I didn't think you'd be the one to hurt them," she said.

Beth gazed at Jena. The woman's expression was angry. "What?"

"Carly and Quinton. I didn't think *you'd* be the one to do it—hurt them. He told me he asked you to marry him. How could you do *this?*" She gestured around the room. "*How could you* rip apart what was obviously such a good thing for everyone?"

Beth folded her hands into her lap. To hear what she'd done harshly put… But what was done, was done, and it would be for the best.

"He's not in love with me," Beth said simply. "I wish things could have been different. But you see, I thought I was in love once, and I trapped my husband because I was pregnant. He married me because of the baby. He resented me for that until the day he died. He loved his daughter, but please, who doesn't love Carly? Quinton would have been the same way. He wanted a family. He wanted my daughter. I just came with the package. I can't marry again just because it's convenient to do so. I need it all, Jena. Carly deserves two parents who have it all, and that means love."

Jena didn't appear convinced. "He's miserable without you. He's even lost weight. He looks terrible," she said.

"Then why didn't he come after me?"

"Because he's one of the proudest men I know. He'll

martyr himself and his desires if he feels living without him is what you want. Perhaps he didn't realize he was in love with you."

Oh, how Beth wished that were true. "He loves me, yes, but only as a friend. He's not *in love* with me. There's a difference. As for him missing me, he probably just feels alone. A person gets used to having someone around. It's hard to let that go. In my life, I've learned that there are worse things than being alone."

"But you aren't alone," Jena argued. "You have Carly."

Beth clenched her hands. "And I have to protect her."

Jena shook her head. "He never would have left you. He never would have hurt you or cheated on you. He would have kept you on a pedestal for all of your days."

"But I can't be someone's roommate and sexual companion. Eventually that kind of relationship ends."

Jena waved her hands in the air. "I would never have taken you for a fool. You have no idea what you've done, do you? You ripped him apart. He won't come crawling back to you. Ever."

"I don't expect him to." Tears threatened, and Beth bit the inside of her lip hard so that they wouldn't start flowing. "My decision was best for everyone. It may not appear like that now, but I know it was."

"I still say you're a fool," Jena told her with another shake of her head. She seemed to want to say more, but at that moment Carly bounded back into the room, her arms loaded with her four other Barbie dolls.

Beth stood. "Excuse me a moment," she said. Busy with the Barbie dolls, neither Jena nor Carly looked up as she left.

The bathroom was tiny, the sink so ancient it had separate faucets for hot and cold water. Beth sat on the toilet lid and bit back tears. Failing in her quest, she let herself have a good cry for the first time since she'd moved out from Quinton's. When her sobs finally subsided, she needed another two minutes to pull herself together. Then she washed her face and headed back.

Carly and Jena were deep in conversation, but both stared up at her when she walked into the room. "Are you okay, Mommy?"

"I'm fine sweetheart," Beth said.

Jena got up. "I have to get going. Beth, do you mind if next week—say, Saturday—I take Carly to the museum? That's the twenty-sixth, I think."

"I want to go, Mommy. I miss Jena."

Beth was about to say no. But did Jena also need to belong to the past? And Carly looked so hopeful. "Okay," Beth said.

"Wonderful," Jena replied. "It's a date, squirt. I'll see you in just a few days."

Carly gave Jena a big hug. "A date," she told Jena. She smiled broadly. "Mommy, I have a date."

Beth laughed. "You do," she said. "A play date with Jena. It's awfully nice of her to take you."

"I know," Carly said. She walked Jena to the door. "Thank you for the Barbie doll. Bye, Jena."

Jena bent down to Carly's level. "Bye, Carly. I'll be

here at ten a.m. next Saturday. If you have a calendar, you can *X* off the days until then."

"We have one of those in the kitchen," Carly said. "May I do it, Mommy?"

"You may," Beth said. She watched Jena and Carly hug and then Jena was gone. Beth spent the rest of the evening wondering if what Jena had said about Quinton was true.

CARLY MARKED the day off on the calendar and headed to her room. Her mommy hadn't seemed very happy to see Jena. But, when Carly thought about it, her mommy hadn't been very happy lately.

Ever since they'd moved into this apartment, Mommy had stopped smiling. Oh, she would be fun occasionally, like today when they'd made pumpkin bread and Carly had gotten batter on her nose. For the most part, though, Mommy wasn't happy.

And that made Carly sad.

Jena said that Carly's mommy had a broken heart. As Carly played with her dolls, she wondered how hearts got broken. Aunt Ida had a broken heart once, and she'd needed to go to the hospital for surgery. Aunt Ida had been gone for a long time.

Carly didn't want her mommy to be gone for a long time. Maybe Cupid could bring Mommy a new heart. Did he work on days besides Valentine's Day? The tooth fairy worked every day. Maybe if she gave up her Easter basket, the Easter bunny would bring her mom a new heart.

Carly thought about that for a while. Maybe Jena would know. Carly decided to ask Jena about it when they went out on their date.

"Carly, time for bed," her mother called.

Carly put her Barbie dolls away. Yes, she would ask Jena. Jena worked at a hospital. Jena would know what to do.

Chapter Twelve

"It was a what?" As Quinton began to tell his mother the truth, Babs really did look ready to have a heart attack.

"A charade. A scam," Quinton repeated. He'd endured his parents' sympathy for far too long if the past twenty-four hours counted. He'd never been good at lying to them, and guilt at deceiving them had been consuming him ever since he'd arrived late last night.

Quinton and his parents had moved into the salon following a family dinner, and his left hand clutched the glass of mineral water as though it were a lifeline. He'd surprised his parents first by coming home pretty much unannounced, and then he'd sprung this on them. He took a deep, cleansing breath and began.

"Beth and I concocted the whole engagement. It wasn't real. Never."

"Please tell me you're lying." Babs's hands shook slightly.

"I wish I could say I was, but then I'd just be lying. I've done enough of that lately," Quinton admitted.

With his free hand he reached into his pocket and extracted the ring box. He set it on the end table. "It started off just as a way to have a date for Shelby's wedding. You were so insistent about Susie and St. Louis. I wanted to buy some time."

As he remembered the ruse, he shook his head. "I did ask Beth to marry me, though. The night of Shelby's wedding. She said no. She moved out the Monday when we got back to Chicago. She left her key and the ring. I haven't talked to her since."

"I think I need to hear the whole story." Babs sat down on the brocade sofa. "Why don't you tell me everything. Start at the beginning."

"I'd like to hear this, too," his father said. He seated himself next to his wife, and Quinton took a seat on the sofa across from them. Facing them was hard, but losing Beth, living without her, was much harder. He hated every moment of it. He hated the pity of his friends and co-workers. He hated Jena's anger most of all, for she had warned him. He also hated the fact that although he knew she'd seen Beth and Carly, his pride prevented him from asking her how they were. But no involvement was the way Beth wanted things, and he was man enough to respect her choice, no matter how much it killed him. He took a drink.

"I met her in the ER, as I told you…" Quinton began. He'd filled them in on all the relevant details, from Beth's fainting to her relenting to the scheme. The only part he left out was the bachelor party and Beth's role in that.

"So you concocted this scheme because you didn't want to return to St. Louis and take over your father's practice?" Babs appeared confused.

Quinton nodded. "I also didn't want to date Susie," he added.

Babs now looked stricken. "Have I really been that insensitive? Beth said something at the reception, but I didn't realize…"

"Don't take this as disrespect, but yes, you have been unbearable. I promised Dad to go easy on you because of your heart condition. I didn't want to stress you."

"Have I been that overbearing?" Babs appeared affronted and then suddenly she slumped in resignation. "I have been. I guess I'm spoiled and I like having my own way. I just wanted you closer. I have been turning a deaf ear to what you want."

"True, but I should have been honest. Having Beth be my fake fiancée seemed like a fine idea, but it backfired." Quinton tapped his finger on the upholstery. "Big-time."

"Thankfully my heart is fine, or the stress of this truth would kill me," Babs said. She sighed. "And I admit that perhaps I overdo it a bit so that I can get what I want. Call it an old lady's prerogative or the prerogative of being the youngest girl in Joan-the-super-sister's family. I don't know. What I do know is that I sure don't plan on leaving this earth anytime soon."

"She's too tenacious to die," Fred added. He gave his wife a kiss on her cheek.

"Exactly," Babs said with a vigorous, life-affirming nod. "So besides that, where do things stand? How do you really feel about Beth?"

He'd thought of nothing else for the past two weeks, analyzing every moment they'd spent together, over and over. "I'm starting to realize that partly I partici-pated in the scheme because deep down, I didn't want Beth to go. I enjoyed having her around and taking care of her. And her daughter is such a doll. When I first pro-posed the arrangement to Beth, she turned it down. I thought it was off. So when you and Shelby showed up on my doorstep, it was as much of a surprise to me as to you that Beth announced we were engaged."

Babs only nodded, which encouraged him to con-tinue.

"It became so real so fast," he said. "We got caught up in the whirlwind. Or at least I did. I kept thinking I could make what wasn't real, real. Beth, though, kept her focus. She saw the deal through to the end and then moved out. She kept telling me it was all a fantasy, that it would end. And it did."

"And you miss her," Fred said.

"Very much," Quinton said.

"So what do you plan on doing?"

"I don't know," Quinton said. "She left me. I have to respect that. She didn't want to marry for conven-ience, and that's what our arrangement was."

"You aren't in love with her?"

"I've been asking myself that question for two weeks. I don't know. I know I have a hole inside of me that aches. I miss her smile. I miss her laugh. I miss talking to her. I want to kiss her, hug her, hold her in my arms and make love to her all night." He flushed suddenly as he realized what he'd just revealed. "I want the pain to go away."

"I'm your mother," Babs said. "It's okay. You're not in high school anymore. Didn't you think I knew you were sneaking around my house?"

"Oh," Quinton said.

"Sounds to me like you're in love with her," Fred said. "The question is, do you want her forever?"

"As I told you, I asked her to marry me," Quinton replied. He'd asked Beth, all right, he'd wanted convenience, safety. She'd been right to turn him down. He hadn't recognized what being in love really was in all its wrappings. He hadn't recognized what he knew now. He really *was* in love with her. He was thirty-five and clueless.

His sister would say "How like a man."

He'd definitely screwed up. The question was what to do about it.

"So what are you going to do about it?" Babs asked, verbalizing his thoughts.

Quinton had long ago set down his mineral water. He reached over to the end table and retrieved the ring box. He opened it and stared at the heirloom ring that had been on Beth's finger. He shut the ring box with a decisive snap and passed the box over to his mother.

"I'm not going to do anything," he said. He couldn't. Beth had made her wishes clear.

Babs set the box on the coffee table. "But if you're in love with her…?"

"I'll set her free the way she's asked me to," Quinton said. "If she comes back…"

His voice faded as he remembered the childhood poster of wild horses Shelby had had in her room. The caption had read: "If you love something, set it free. If it comes back to you, it's yours. If it doesn't, it wasn't meant to be."

And he had to admit that it would seem pretty hollow if he showed up now, declared what a fool he'd been and told Beth he was in love with her. Even if she did love him back, she'd told him she couldn't live in his world. Her pride and determination outdid his, and no matter what, he'd respect her decision. He wanted her to be happy, and if that meant without him, so be it.

She'd rejected him once. He couldn't bear it again.

"You know what's best," Fred said. "We raised you to do the right thing. We won't sit in judgment of your decision."

"We'll support you in whatever you do," Babs added.

"Thanks." Quinton gazed around the room. He'd been running away from home for so long, but now that he needed his parents and home, both were right there for him. "I may move back here and take over that practice of yours, Dad. That is, if the offer is still open."

"You're welcome to do that, son, but you don't have to," Fred said. He reached over and held his wife's hand. "I never meant for you to feel pressured to follow in my footsteps. I have plenty of partners who will be more than happy to buy me out. You've created your own life. You don't have to take over mine."

"I understand that now," Quinton said. "But still let me think about it for a day or two. Chicago doesn't hold the appeal it once did. I see her everywhere—you know?"

Babs nodded. "And I want you to be happy. If it's here in St. Louis, I'll be the happiest mother in the world. And I promise I won't play matchmaker."

Quinton managed a wry smile. Odds were his mother would last about a week with that resolution. "Mind if I go upstairs? I'm pretty beat and I haven't been feeling quite myself lately."

"We don't mind," his mother said. "Do you want us to stay home tonight? We could play cards or something."

"No," Quinton said with a shake of his head. "Don't stay away from Bob and Joan's and your bridge game on my account. Just send them my love."

With that, he left his parents and headed upstairs.

A FEW DAYS LATER, he still hadn't decided what to do, although he knew that the apartment he'd once loved now stifled. Even its north and east views of the wintry Lake Michigan did little to soothe his aching heart.

No, it was obvious that he might as well go home to St. Louis. Heck, when he felt up for it, maybe he could do that It's Just Lunch dating service or something. Perhaps even let his mother play matchmaker.

The thought did little to cheer him. But Chicago, which had once seemed so freeing, now seemed unbearable without Beth.

"Boy, you're a sourpuss," Jena remarked one evening in March as they worked a graveyard shift together in the ER. "What's eating you, as if I couldn't guess."

"I'm going back to St. Louis," he said. "I talked to my father. I'm taking over his pediatric practice. We're thinking a summer transition would be best."

"You're moving?" Jena put down the chart she'd been holding. She shoved her hand into her teddy bear coat. "What possessed you to do that? Wasn't that whole dumb idea of yours so you wouldn't have to go?"

"It's time. Returning to St. Louis isn't as horrible an idea as I once thought," Quinton said. He picked up the phone so he could update the pediatrician about the girl in room seven. "I'm putting my condo on the market in April, and I'll sell my sailboat. There aren't any lakes around St. Louis large enough for it. I probably won't have much time for sailing, anyway."

Jena stared at him as if he'd grown two heads. "What about Beth?" Jena asked. "You fell in love with her when she moved in and I doubt it's changed now that she's moved out. You need to talk to her. You're crazy if you don't. I've seen her twice, and she's not doing any better than you. Lower your pride for once. One of you has to."

So *now* Jena tells him how Beth has been doing.

Quinton gave Jena a sad smile. "Beth and I are over," he said. "Beth was right—we are from two different worlds. She went back to hers and I'm going back to mine."

"But your feelings—"

Quinton held up his hand to stop Jena. "It's over. We're both going on with our lives. Now, I have to make this call." He put the receiver to his ear and began dialing.

Jena simply shook her head, picked up the chart and walked away.

Chapter Thirteen

"Jena, do you keep hearts at the hospital where you work?"

Jena glanced up at Carly in surprise. Since they'd had such fun on their date the previous weekend, Beth had let Jena have Carly for an encore. Thus, the two of them had spent the day at the Museum of Science and Industry, and then for a treat Jena had taken Carly to American Girl Place. They were sitting in the café, having a bite to eat before Jena headed to the hospital for a Saturday-night shift.

"What do you mean, do we keep hearts at the hospital?"

"New hearts to fix the broken ones," Carly said.

"Why do you ask that?"

"Because my mommy's heart is broken and Cupid's day is over so he can't bring her a new one," Carly said. "When my aunt Ida's heart broke she went in the hospital and got a new one."

"She had a heart transplant?"

That didn't sound right. "No, but they fixed it,"

Carly said. "If my mommy goes to the hospital, can they fix her heart?"

Jena's hand paused above her sandwich. There was one person at the hospital who could fix Beth's heart. And fix his own in the process.

"Can Quinton fix my mommy's heart?" Carly continued before she wiped her lips on her napkin like good little girls should. "I miss Quinton. I thought he was going to be my daddy."

"I don't know, honey. You'd have to ask your mommy."

Carly hated those kind of grown-up answers. She stuck out her jaw and stared at her napkin. The cookie had been decorated with Red Hots candy and the white napkin contained traces of red. "She won't talk about it," Carly said.

"I wish I could help you, squirt, but I can't," Jena said. She glanced at her watch. "Let's get you home, shall we? I'm working tonight and I can't be late."

"Okay," Carly said.

Hours later, after dinner and after Ken had kissed Barbie and mended *her* heart, Carly sat down and thought about her mom. Grown-ups were so silly sometimes. Like lipstick. Why would anyone want to wear stuff that came off on other people's faces? Carly frowned as an idea danced just outside her head. The Red Hots candy she'd eaten today had made her lips red… Some candy made your tongue blue… The medicine she'd eaten the day she'd met Quinton had made her mouth green…

To fix her broken heart, her mommy needed Quinton. That much Carly knew. Quinton was at the hospital. Hearts were fixed at the hospital. She just had to get her mommy there.

SATURDAY-NIGHT TELEVISION was boring, Beth thought as she channel-surfed her way through the Chicago stations. She frowned. Even watching mindless TV didn't take her mind off the fact that her independence wasn't all that she'd envisioned it to be.

She missed Quinton. Did he miss her?

She gave her head a vigorous shake. She didn't need to even speculate about that. If he'd wanted to talk, he would have contacted her earlier. Besides, Jena had told her just the other day, when she'd picked up Carly, that Quinton was moving to St. Louis. So much for the original purpose of their fake engagement. He'd decided to take over his father's practice after all.

She wasn't sure how she felt about Quinton's decision. Partly it made a mockery of all they'd been through together. So much for their original purpose— although by his making love with her and then asking her to really marry him the rules had been changed anyway.

But Quinton leaving Chicago? Selling his beloved sailboat? They would never see each other again, which meant that he had let her go, just as she'd asked him to do. The actions, all because of her choice, remained bittersweet.

She missed him, but she had to go on with her life, just as she'd planned.

Even Carly was doing better living somewhere other than Quinton's apartment. She seemed to have adjusted to their new place, at least. Right now she was playing in her room. Beth had a half hour before bed. Since snow and wind blustered outside, she'd made herself a mug of hot chocolate, the kind with the dehydrated marshmallows that puffed up in the hot water. Beth took a drink, and a bit of the marshmallow clung to her top lip. She wiped it with a napkin. A Chicago weatherman had come on the air to say something about a winter weather advisory. The last of his report, however, was interrupted by the sound of a crash in Beth's bedroom.

Beth jumped to her feet, tossed the afghan hastily aside and raced into her bedroom. Her purse had fallen from the top closet shelf. Carly sat on the floor, the up-ended contents strewn all around her.

"Carly, are you all right?"

Carly turned away from her mother. Beth instantly knew that while her daughter was not hurt, something was not right. The little girl was up to something. A broom lay on the floor nearby. "Carly, what are you doing?"

"Nothing," Carly mumbled.

Beth leaned down and grabbed her daughter's arm. She pivoted Carly around. A red line ringed her lips. "What did you do?"

"Nothing," Carly insisted again.

"Answer me!" Beth's voice rose to a shout. She sank to her knees and began digging through the mess on the floor. She didn't own lipstick that shade of red. "What did you eat? Tell me, Carly. What did you eat?"

"Candy—" Carly answered.

She stuck out her tongue and Beth could see it was bright red.

"Like the Red Hots on the cookies today."

"Where did you get red candy?" Beth said. She reached for Carly's clenched hand, and peeled it open and pulled out a medicine packet. Her hand shook. "No. You did not eat these. These are not Red Hots. These are not candy."

"Red Hots," Carly said stubbornly. "*S* for *sweet*."

"These aren't Red Hots," Beth repeated. Desperation filled her. This was not happening again. Her daughter couldn't have… "These are medicine, Carly. Pills for Mommy. How many of these did you take? This package only holds two."

Carly shifted slightly and Beth saw more sets of the medicine wrappers. Beth's fingernails scraped the wrappers up from the worn brown carpet. If Carly had eaten all of them, she'd ingested over ten of the small red decongestant pills.

Dear Lord, not again. She rose to her feet. "Let's get dressed, sweetie. We must go now."

"Go where?" Carly asked as she stood up.

"The hospital."

Carly stared at the floor. "Am I dying?"

Beth surely hoped not. "No, honey. You might have to drink that special drink again, though."

"Don't wanna," Carly said. She looked up and stomped her foot. "They were candy."

"Don't argue with me. These are medicine packets, not candy wrappers, and that means we need to go, *now!*"

"I wanna bring my purse," Carly said. She pointed to a pink purse decorated with a pony.

"Fine," Beth said. Carly could grab anything as long as she got moving. Beth dressed Carly in a heavy winter coat and snow boots, and within minutes they were on the L. Luck was with Beth, for when she and Carly reached street level, the snow flurries had stopped and she was easily able to hail a cab to take them the rest of the way to the hospital.

"No more drink stuff," Carly said when she saw the sign for Chicago Presbyterian. "No, Mommy. No."

"We don't have a choice," Beth said.

Minutes later she pushed her way into the ER. Surprisingly, only a few people were in the waiting room—maybe they all showed up after midnight, when the bars began to close. Right now it didn't matter. Beth signed in at the counter, and within moments the triage nurse called them back.

"How many pills?" the ER nurse asked.

"Ten," Beth said. "At least ten. The container only holds two. I counted the wrappers she'd tossed on the ground."

The nurse made some notations. "Please have a seat

in the waiting room. Someone from Pediatrics will be right down to get you."

"Thanks." Urgency mixed with raw fear gripped Beth. She held Carly tight in her arms. Her daughter was falling asleep. That wasn't a good sign, was it? Beth didn't know. "Wake up, honey. Look. Watch the television with Mommy. I'll let you stay up late. Come on, sweetheart, wake up."

"Uh-huh," Carly murmured.

"Carly Johnson? Beth?" Jena appeared in the ER doorway. She wore her teddy bear nurse's coat.

"Jena, thank God." Beth stood up, her child a heavy load. "She's sleeping, Jena. Is that okay? She took so many pills. Is she going to be all right?"

"Let's get her upstairs," Jena said.

Beth followed Jena and the elevator ride to the pediatric floor seemed to take forever.

"In here," Jena said. The room was a different one from the butterfly room they'd been in before. This one was decorated with teddy bears. Jena drew the privacy curtain over the glass window that overlooked the nurses' station.

Beth laid Carly on the patient bed. "It'll be okay, Beth," Jena said. "Why don't you go down the hall to the left and splash some water on your face? Go on."

As Beth left the room, Carly glanced up at Jena.

"Did you take those pills?" Jena asked.

"No," Carly said with a shake that sent her pigtails flying. Jena began to check Carly's vital signs. "Mommy needs a new heart. I had to get her here to get one. She hates hospitals. She won't come on her own. So I got in her purse and found her medicine. I licked on it and painted my lips. All the pills are in here." Carly patted her purse.

"You did a foolish thing," Jena said as she inspected the purse.

Carly's lips quivered. She didn't want Jena to be angry at her. "I'm so sorry," she managed to say. "But Mommy needs Quinton to give her a new heart. He's the only one who can."

Jena ruffled Carly's hair for a moment. "You're probably right, but what you did was wrong."

"I know."

"You have to tell your mommy. She's very worried."

"I will."

"She's here now," Jena said as Beth reentered the room. Jena removed the stethoscope from her ears. "I'm going to get the doctor. Carly, talk to your mom."

"Okay," Carly said as her mother moved over to sit on the bed by her.

"So what are you to tell me?" Beth asked. She glanced at the clock and saw it was a little past ten.

"I love you, Mommy," Carly said. "I was wrong."

"I love you, sweetie. But I thought you would have learned the first time. You don't take Mommy's medicine."

"I did learn," Carly said with a nod. She glanced toward the door. "Do you think Quinton is here?"

"No, sweetie. I'm sure he has somewhere else to be.

He's moving back to St. Louis. We probably won't be seeing him again."

"You should have married him, Mommy," Carly said. "I love him and he could give you a new heart to fix your broken one. You can get your heart fixed in a hospital. Here we are. I'm sorry for what I did."

He had given her a new heart, Beth thought. She had just been too foolish to realize it. She'd also been too stubborn to admit her mistake. Perhaps she should have called him, even if only to see how he was. She gazed at the closed curtain.

"He has to be here, Mommy. He has to fix your heart. Oh, and I didn't eat any pills. See? They're right here in my purse."

QUINTON WAS STANDING at the nurses' desk and he looked up as Jena approached. "Your drug overdose is here. I took vitals. Everything appears to be normal, nothing out of the ordinary at all," she said.

"Okay." He paused a moment to rub the back of his neck, then went to a small sink and washed his hands. So far the pediatric ER had been slow. Downstairs had been, too, although Quinton knew the graveyard shift would be busy later.

As he walked toward room one, he frowned. Jena had drawn the curtains. He stepped through the doorway and froze. As his brain registered Beth's and Carly's presence, he hoped that the sight was a mirage. Anger consumed him when he realized it wasn't. He lashed out before he could check his temper.

"You let her do it again, Beth? How could you be so irresponsible?"

"I—" Beth's lips trembled and tears flowed. "My purse was on the top shelf of my closet. She used a broom handle to pull it down. I just learned she didn't really take the medicine. It's in her purse…."

"Carly, we talked about this," Quinton said sternly, so angry that he didn't even hear what Beth had said. His hands trembled and he clenched them into fists. She was a patient. He was supposed to be impassive, impersonal. Compassionate, yes, yet not involved.

But he *was* personally involved.

Oh, to hell with pretending otherwise. He cared. He cared way too much. He loved this child and had wanted to be her father. He would deal with her mother and this indiscretion of hers later. That was a certainty.

"Carly, we said no more eating medicine."

Jena stepped into the doorway and Carly's gaze found hers. "I showed Mommy, Jena," she said. "See, all the pills are in my purse." Carly dumped the purse out and ten little red pills fell on the hospital bed.

"You must tell the truth, Carly," Quinton said. "You could be very sick if you don't."

Carly nodded. "I licked one and painted my mouth. See, it's white. The rest are all red and right here."

"What?" Quinton said. "Is this some sort of a joke?" Beth still looked shell-shocked, as if not believing Carly could be capable of such a stunt. He turned to Jena. She'd already stepped forward and scooped Carly up into her arms.

"No joke," she said. "A wake-up call from a little girl who thinks that you're the only one who can fix her mom's broken heart. I've scolded her for the stunt, and I'm sure Beth will, as well. But, even though Carly was wrong in what she did, why don't you do what she wanted? Take this chance to make things right. Rogers came in already. You and Beth love each other. For once, both of you don't be stubborn or stupid, and use this time to talk. Carly and I are going to go get something to eat and then watch some television. Don't blow it."

"Jena," Quinton began, but Jena lifted her chin in defiance and walked out with Carly.

"Oh, my," Beth said.

Quinton turned and gazed at her. Her elbows were on her knees and her head in her hands. "I didn't know about this. I thought she'd really taken them. I didn't know she was smart enough to pull a stunt like this. She's smart, but…I didn't think she'd even do something like this."

He could see that she hadn't known. As he studied her, he realized that Jena was right. Beth looked like hell. While she appeared healthier than the last time she'd been in the ER, that night he'd first met her, she didn't necessarily seem any better. Not that she wasn't beautiful. To him, Beth would always be beautiful. But there were stress lines on her face now, stress lines from being tired of life, stress lines from not being as happy as she'd been when she'd lived with him.

Her inner fire, the passion that was so Beth, had been extinguished.

"How've you been?" he said lamely.

"Fine," Beth replied, once again giving him her standard answer.

"You're always fine," he said wryly, and couldn't help smiling. "I've discovered that about you. The invincible Beth Johnson is always fine."

"I have to be," she said. "And I'm sorry this happened. When Jena took Carly to the museum today Carly had cookies with Red Hots on them. That's the only explanation I can come up with. This is not where I wanted to be on a Saturday night."

"Let's see if I can guess what you were doing. Tonight you were hanging out with the TV."

She didn't reply, but he could see in her blue eyes that he was right. Oh, how he adored her eyes, especially when he had stared into them during their long lovemaking sessions. "Don't be embarrassed. It's not like I have anything more exciting to do. I always do an ER shift on Saturdays. Someone has to."

"Well, I'll scold her a great deal for this," Beth said. She sat up straight, her arms falling to her sides.

She was slipping away from him, ready to angle for an escape. Jena had said not to blow it, and Quinton knew he was close to doing just that.

"What about pastry school? Did you enroll in your classes?" he asked quickly.

"I decided to wait," Beth said. "But Nancy gave me a bonus. I'm out of debt. So maybe next fall when Carly starts kindergarten I'll enroll in more classes."

"She'll be in public school?"

"I can't afford private," Beth said.

Her spine stiffened, an almost imperceptible movement that he perceived only because he understood her so well.

"But maybe I'll check into scholarships. There might be some private schools. With this stunt she has certainly proven that she can act." She grinned.

"She's sharp…I've missed her," he added gently. The words came from the depths of his heart. Beth's eyes grew cloudy and she turned away. Quinton stepped over to her, he reached out and lifted her chin. Her skin felt smooth and silky. "I've missed *you*," he said.

Oh, please don't say that! Beth's heart cried out. And then his gaze locked onto hers. Maybe this was the time for a new beginning. No lies, no fake engagements, nothing but another chance for happiness.

"I've missed you." Her voice was barely above a whisper.

"I know," he said. "We were good together."

All she could do was nod.

"We belong together."

Beth opened her mouth, but anticipating her movement, Quinton lifted his fingers from her chin and silenced her lips. "I told my parents the whole truth," he said. "All of it. Well, minus the bachelor party. But I told them about how I thought up with this dumb idea, and how you disagreed, but then how you rode to my defense and saved me when my mother showed up. I told my parents that I'd asked you to marry me. I told them that I didn't want you to go. I've hated every day that has passed since you left me."

She tried to speak, but he shook his head.

"I don't want this to be like some soap opera where things go unsaid. Hear me out. Then you can yell, scream, whatever."

Beth nodded.

He smiled. "My mother asked me if I loved you. And perhaps it took your actually walking out on me to make me realize that my life without you is nothing. I don't want my boat. I don't want my condo. I don't want anything but you. I searched my soul and concluded that I am in love with you. Because you are you. I'm in love with you, heart and soul. Everything that goes with it. You are all I want. You, me, Carly. And not because I can't be alone. Not because I need a roommate. But because you complete me."

He stepped back and removed his fingers from her lips. "You're free, which is what you asked for. That's why I didn't come find you, come after you and beg you for forgiveness and another chance."

"I…" Yes, she'd asked to be free. But if he was in love with her the way she'd wanted him to be…? Did three little words change everything? No. She'd changed. She'd realized she was wrong. She'd missed him, period. They had not admitted what was in front of them. If he'd asked her to return, even without love, she'd have done it. He was haggard. The past weeks showed in the stress on his face. And truth shone in his eyes.

"I was wrong," she said. "What we had was enough before I left. I threw it away. Pride, perhaps. My old patterns of behavior. You are not anything like Randy. I should never have painted you with that same brush. I…I love you, Quinton."

And there it was. Out.

He stared at her. "Why did we do this to each other?"

Her brow furrowed in confusion. "Do what?"

"Why did we waste all this time?" he asked. "If Carly hadn't concocted this scheme of hers…" His voice trailed off.

She gave him a sad smile. "She wanted to get me to the hospital so I could get my broken heart fixed. We're adults. I would think we were smarter than this."

"I guess we weren't. We're lucky Carly is smarter than the two of us together. Of course, we are going to have to punish her, but we'll talk about that later. I love you, Beth Johnson. Don't leave me again."

"I won't," she promised.

"Seal it with a kiss," Quinton said, and he brought his lips down on hers.

Beth reveled in his kiss, a kiss that tasted of promise for now and ever after.

He withdrew his lips, a wistful smile on his face. "This room is not the place to continue that kiss."

"No," she agreed.

"You know, they say the person whose life you save is the one you must stay with forever," he said. "You're going to have to get used to me."

Beth smiled. "I think I can manage."

Quinton's grin matched her own. "Good, because we'll be together no matter what. Although I plan on kissing you every minute from here on out, just to be certain. How about we gather up Carly and go home?"

"I think I'd like that," Beth said. She followed Quinton out into the hallway. Jena and Carly were approaching, Carly with a candy bar in her hand.

"I see that's highly nutritious," Quinton said.

Jena gave him a shrug and simply ignored him.

"So are you going to marry my mommy?" Carly asked. "You're the only one who can fix her broken heart."

Quinton turned so he could face Beth. "If she'll have me, my offer to marry your mommy still stands. I think I've made the offer a bit better this time. I love your mommy and she's the only one to fix *my* heart."

His words said it all, and Beth's heart overflowed. She loved this man. "You *have* come up with a better offer and I think that this time I'll say yes," Beth replied. "My heart now and forever belongs to you."

Carly tugged on Jena's arm. "What are they saying?" she asked.

"Their hearts are fixed," Jena said. "It means you did good, squirt, although I still have a feeling that you're going to get grounded."

"We're also saying it's time to go home and be a family," Quinton said. "I love your mommy, she loves me and we both love you. How about that?"

"Yes!" Carly danced around, not too worried at the

moment about any upcoming reprimand. "I'm getting a daddy," she shouted. "I'm getting a daddy!"

"Who never wants to see a stunt like this out of you again," Quinton said.

Carly stopped dancing. A ring of chocolate surrounded her mouth. "I promise," she said with a solemn nod. Then Carly brightened. "I'm going to be a flower girl. I'm going to be a flower girl!"

Quinton reached for Beth, put his arm around her and drew her close.

He brought his mouth to hers and captured her lips in a passionate kiss, but pulled back slightly as he heard Carly say, "Are they always going to kiss like that?"

"Get used to it," Jena said.

And even though he heard Carly and Jena, Quinton's gaze was locked onto Beth's. He raised his hands to her lips and kissed the back of her hand. "I love you," he said. "I always will."

Beth nodded, the words she wanted to say lost in another kiss.

But Quinton knew what she couldn't say. He drew back, his gaze holding hers. "I didn't make a New Year's resolution this year, but believe me, it's to love you forever."

"Mine, too," Beth said as tears of happiness ran down her cheeks. She'd found her prince, and he'd made her a princess. They loved each other, and together their future looked bright. With love, it always and forever would be.

Epilogue

"What is it with the women in this family being pregnant before they're married?" Babs threw her hands in the air. "I guess you'll use the excuse that you've been living together, too."

Quinton shrugged, the tux rising and falling with his shoulders. "Yeah, well, Grandma, get used to it."

"Shelby's showing and you're…" Babs waved a hand in front of her face as if the room had suddenly gotten too hot. "And I'm still going to work on you two moving to St. Louis. Beth can finish school here, and I want my grandchildren here."

"It's time for us to sit down," Fred said. He gave Quinton a knowing glance and guided his wife out of the narthex and up the aisle to the family pew.

Quinton grinned. He and Beth hadn't wanted a large wedding, but they'd let Babs overrule them. What she'd pulled off in just a short period of time was amazing. Quinton didn't mind at all the fanfare. He'd wanted Beth to have a wedding with all the trimmings that she'd never had the first time around. He wanted their late-June marriage memories to be totally different from those of her courthouse ceremony to Randy. Thus, they were being married in the same Kirkwood, Missouri, church that Alan and Shelby had been married in.

At the appropriate time, Quinton took his place at the front of the church. The minister gave him a smile and the music changed.

The flower girl came first. She wore a short-sleeved white gown, white hose and white Mary Jane shoes. She strode forward a few steps and tossed out some red rose petals. Then she stopped, turned around and grabbed her mother's hand.

Quinton's heart swelled as he watched the woman he loved approach. Her dress was a simple ivory creation, and the hairstylist had woven white flowers into her hair. Although Beth's pregnancy did not yet show, Quinton already loved the little one growing inside her. This was his family. He was indeed blessed.

Carly didn't falter this time, but escorted her mother the entire way down the aisle, coming to stop at the steps leading to the altar.

Quinton met them there. He leaned over and kissed Carly on the cheek as she held out her mommy's hand the way they'd practiced the night before.

"Good job," he told her.

Carly skipped into the front pew and sat by Babs.

Quinton took Beth's hand and she linked her arm through his. Her blue eyes misted. "Ready?" he asked. They would walk to the altar together.

She nodded. "I love you," she said.

"Then walk with me forever," he said. "Be my wife."

Beth nodded. "I will."

Hearing her words and seeing the love in her eyes, Quinton felt a joy such as he had never known. Fate had given him this woman, given them this moment. Arms linked, they made their way forward together, one step at a time, into their future.

* * * * *

Turn the page to read excerpts from next month's Harlequin American Romance selections. You'll find a range of stories and styles. In March, we're offering books from some of your favorite authors—Judy Christenberry, Leah Vale and Linda Randall Wisdom— and from newcomer Lisa McAllister, a delightful new addition to our lineup.

The Marine by Leah Vale
(Harlequin American Romance 1057)

This is the third title in Leah Vale's miniseries THE
LOST MILLIONAIRES. In these books, four men—
the secret offspring of millionaire Joseph McCoy's son,
Marcus—are contacted by the family's lawyers. Mar-
cus is dead—and his sons are now millionaires....
You'll enjoy this fast-paced, humorous and yet emo-
tional story! (And watch for the fourth book, *The Rich
Boy* in May.)

Dear Major Branigan,
It is our duty at this time to inform you of the
death of Marcus McCoy due to an unfortunate,
unforeseen encounter with a grizzly bear while
fly-fishing in Alaska on June 8 of this year, and
per the stipulations set forth in his last will and
testament, to make formal his acknowledgment
of one USMC Major Rick Thomas Branigan,

age 33, 7259 Villa Crest Drive, #12, Oceanedge, California, as being his son and heir to an equal portion of his estate.

It is the wish of Joseph McCoy, father to Marcus McCoy, grandfather to Rick Branigan, and founder of McCoy Enterprises, that you immediately assume your rightful place in the family home and business with all due haste and utmost discretion to preserve the family's privacy.

Regards,

David Weidman, Esq.

Weidman, Biddermier, Stark

"My life just keeps getting better and better," Major Rick Branigan grumbled at the letter he held in one hand....

Rachel's Cowboy by Judy Christenberry
(Harlequin American Romance 1058)

Rachel's Cowboy is the next installment in Judy Christenberry's popular new series CHILDREN OF TEXAS. You'll find Judy's trademark warmth here, and her strong sense of family and community—not to mention her love for Texas, her home state!

A Soldier's Return, the next CHILDREN OF TEXAS story, appears in July 2005.

For the first time in her life Rachel Barlow had time on her hands.

After working nonstop for the past six months, she stood in Vivian and Will Greenfield's spacious home feeling at loose ends, trying to rest. She didn't know how. Her constant worries and her hectic schedule had caused her to lose weight. Still, she couldn't stop fretting about her future.

Thanks to her adoptive mother, who'd stolen all Rachel's savings and even borrowed money in her name, she'd been forced to take on one modeling assignment after another, with the hope of repaying the debt and building a nest egg. But she was about to crack.

Her two sisters—Vanessa Shaw, Vivian's adopted daughter, and Rebecca Jacobs, who was Rachel's twin—were concerned about her. They'd persuaded her to move into Vivian's home, where she could be taken care of.

She looked around the lavish Highland Park home that after six months she still wasn't used to. It was strange not only living in such luxury, but also having a loving family.

When the doorbell chimed, she called out, "I'll get it." Knowing the housekeeper would be in the kitchen, she figured she'd save Betty the trip.

She swung open the door and stared at the one man she'd never wanted to see again.

J. D. Stanley.

Frozen with horror, she said nothing.

Neither did he.

Then, when he took a step toward her, cowboy hat in hand, she asked, "What are *you* doing here?"

At the same time he demanded, "What are *you* doing here?"

Neither of them answered.

Single Kid Seeks Dad by Linda Randall Wisdom
(Harlequin American Romance 1059)

Clever, fast-paced and charming, this is a story about
matchmakers—with a difference. Take one young boy
with a single mother and one older man with a single
son and see what kind of plan they come up with!

A delightful story that's guaranteed to make you
smile.

The small, dimly lit room was a dark contrast to the
bright lights and merriment going on in the nearby reception hall. It was the perfect meeting place for the
two conspirators who faced each other.

"I have to say, young man, that your note was in-
triguing. Are you now going to reveal why we're having this meeting in private?" The older man settled
back in a chair and studied the boy facing him. He was
impressed that even with the stern eye he kept on him,
the kid didn't waver.

"It's very simple." The boy kept his voice low. "I have a single mom. You have a single son. We both want to see them married off. There's no reason we can't work together to accomplish our objectives."

The man chuckled. "I suppose you have a plan?"

"Yes, I do. We're already ahead, because your son's hot for my mom."

The older man shook his head. "I've also heard that she's told him she isn't interested."

The boy shrugged off his statement. "Yeah, but that can change. I did some research on your son, and what I've learned tells me he's perfect for my mom. All she needs is some time to really get to know him."

The man chuckled. "How do you expect to bring them together?"

Nick Donner smiled. "I worked up what I feel is a foolproof plan." He then proceeded to explain the idea.

The older man's skepticism soon turned to interest as he listened to Nick. "I'll admit that I'm impressed. Do you honestly think something that wild could work?"

"There is absolutely no reason it won't, as long as you're willing to do your part," Nick said with unshakable confidence.

An hour later their plan was mutually agreed upon with a handshake. The two participants slipped out of the room separately and returned to the reception hall just in time to watch Nora Summers Walker and her new husband, Mark Walker, cut the wedding cake.

For the balance of the evening the young man and

his older partner didn't do anything to betray that they had come up with a plan that if successfully carried out meant another wedding would occur in the near future. That of Lucy Donner and Judge Kincaid's son, Logan.

The Baby Season by Lisa McAllister
(Harlequin American Romance 1060)

Welcome to Halden, North Dakota! This small prairie
town has always been home to midwife Gen Hal-
vorson. Veterinarian Josh McBride and his son, Tyler,
are new here—and despite his differences with Gen,
Josh soon finds himself falling for her.

You'll be enchanted by Lisa McAllister's characters.
And you'll enjoy visiting Halden and its nearby
ranches. This is American country life at its best!

"Dr. Connolly said you're a midwife. What's a midwife?" Tyler asked from the back seat.

Josh answered before Gen had a chance to reply.
"It's a person who helps ladies have their babies."

"Do you do anything else besides help ladies have
babies?" Tyler directed this question at Gen.

"Well, helping deliver babies keeps me pretty busy,"
she replied, "but I'm also an herbalist."

"Oh, that explains it," Josh murmured as Tyler asked, "What's a herbalist?"

"Explains what?" Gen turned to Josh, puzzled. To Tyler she said, "An herbalist is someone who uses plants to make medicines for people and animals." She looked back at Josh, waiting for an answer.

"Are you into all that New Age-y junk or just giving people false hope when there's nothing that can be done?"

Where had that come from? Gen wondered. She bristled at the implication that she was some sort of charlatan. "It's hardly New Age, Dr. McBride. Midwives and herbalists have been around a lot longer than doctors and veterinarians."

"So have witch doctors," he said coolly.

Gen had encountered such bias before. This was the first time, though, that she'd felt compelled to defend herself. What was it about him that made her want to change his mind?

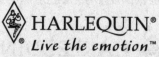

If you enjoyed what you just read,
then we've got an offer you can't resist!

Take 2 bestselling love stories FREE!

Plus get a FREE surprise gift!

Harlequin Romance ®

Contract
Brides

From paper marriage...to wedded bliss?

A wedding dilemma:

What should a sexy, successful bachelor do if he's too busy
making millions to find a wife? Or if he finds the perfect
woman, and just has to strike a bridal bargain...?

The perfect proposal:

The solution? For better, for worse, these grooms in a hurry
have decided to sign, seal and deliver the ultimate
marriage contract...to buy a bride!

Coming soon to

HARLEQUIN ®
Romance ®

in favorite miniseries Contract Brides:

A WIFE ON PAPER
by award-winning author Liz Fielding, #3837
on sale March 2005

VACANCY: WIFE OF CONVENIENCE
by Jessica Steele, #3839
on sale April 2005

Available wherever Harlequin books are sold.

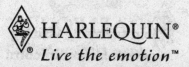

HARLEQUIN ®
® *Live the emotion* ™

www.eHarlequin.com

HRCB

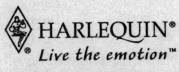